SILENT NIGHT, DEADLY NIGHT

JUDITH CAMPBELL

~Fine. Line. Press~

THE MEDIA

≈

≈

Silent Night…Deadly Night
The second Viridienne Greene Mystery
By
Judith Campbell

~Fine. Line. Press~

Published in the United States of America
~Fine. Line. Press~
Highland Terrace
Plymouth, Massachusetts, 02360
www.judithcampbell-holymysteries.com

ACKNOWLEDGMENTS

Profound thanks to Chris Stokes, AKA Frederick in another life, husband and first reader extraordinaire, Pamela Kelley, best next-door neighbor, author in her own right, www.pamelakelley.com, technical and content advisor, Judie Ivie, editor and friend, and my fellow and sister Scribblers. Without you, this book would NOT be a reality. Thank you.

To my readers. You ask me questions. You challenge me. You encourage me. You NAG me! And you keep me writing. Thank you

PREFACE

There is more to all of this than a word
Or a place
Or even time
That can tell us
What a life meant to be.
What it is that drives the wind
And moves the tides
According to an ancient plan.
Born long before our knowing.
Is it all the one creative, You/Thou/Me, of life,
That brings a grown man to his knees
for love
Breathes life into a child at birth
And shuts the eyes of the newly dead.
Forever?
And do I really need to know.
It will be enough
To be present to the miracle of the ordinary

To sing praises to the everyday.
And say yes to all that is.

PROLOGUE

Breaking news

The body found on the rocks off South Point in Plymouth has been identified as David Nevins, a well-known and highly respected member of Plymouth's LGBTQ community. The death is considered to be a homicide, and a full investigation is underway. Because it is an open case, any further details about the murder itself or information about the investigation is considered confidential and will not be released. However, anyone having any information pertinent to this incident is encouraged to contact Detective Fitzpatrick at Plymouth Police Headquarters.

1

You have mail.

Hi, Lorna Jean. This is a real long shot, but I saw your name and your picture on Facebook, and I think we went to high school together. My name is Richard Correriera. I was Ricky back then. I hope you don't mind me contacting you. I work for the government, and I'll be living out of the country for the next 2 years. My wife died a couple of years ago, and my children are grown and living back in the states. It gets lonely here, especially since it's just me and a dog that followed me home one day from the market place. I'm just looking for a pen pal, nothing more, just someone to write to in the long empty hours away from home.

I was a senior, and you were a sophomore, and back then that was two different worlds. But that could be a story for another time.

If you are the Lorna Jean I went to high school with, I hope we can maybe be FB friends? Just on-line internet pen-pals. I live too far away to ask you out on a date, and I'm not looking for that, just a friend I can talk to. Do you think we can make it happen?

Yours truly, Ricky Jamieson

Hi, Ricky, I think I remember the name, at least it sounds familiar, but I don't think we ever met. Are you sure we went to the same high school?

Hi, Lorna Jean, you can't be sure of anything anymore these days, can you? It's a good thing to ask. It was Longmeadow Regional. I remember the headmaster/principal was named Dr. Orton, and Miss Sharkey taught Spanish. She was the best. Everybody loved her. Does this sound familiar?

I don't believe this, that's the place all right. So where did your family live when you were in school?

We lived on Calumet Ave...where did you live?

Lexington Ave, number 22, but I don't think the house is there anymore.

Ok, now I can't believe this. I used to walk down that street on the way to school. Of course, those were the days before everyone had cars and kids still knew how to walk. Oops, time to go to work, but let's make it happen. I'll try and get back to you later today. TTYL

THE MAN SITTING at the computer clapped his hands together, bookmarked the page and said, "Score." Then he did a couple of neck and shoulder rolls to loosen up after sitting for so long hunched over his laptop. He was getting hungry, but he still had to finish his daily check-in with his three open accounts. After that he'd break for a quick lunch and take a short walk around the block to stretch his legs and get some fresh air in his lungs. Then it was straight back to work. It had been a good morning work-wise, and the man who was about to eat a tuna sandwich with extra cheese and pickle was justifiably pleased with the results of his efforts.

HELLO AGAIN, Lorna Jean,

I hope you don't think I'm going to be pestering you, but I just can't get over the fact that the pretty face I found on a computer screen from half a world away is someone I went to school with. As I said in my first email, I work for the government (Read between the lines!) so I can't say what I do or where I'm doing it, and because of the nature of what I do, I don't have any kind of fixed schedule. I guess that's a long way around of saying that there will be times I won't be able to answer an email as quickly as I would like. So if we do start writing, and I hope we will, and I don't answer right away, I haven't fallen off the face of the earth, I'm just off on a job. Hoping to hear back from you real soon. Let's make it happen.

Yours truly, Rick

I t was early in December, and Viridienne Greene and her sister, Emily Rose Spencer, were seated at the kitchen table finishing breakfast when the house phone rang. They'd been living together for some time now, but they were still getting to know each other.

Within the last year Viridienne had learned she was the new owner of a multi-roomed Victorian home in downtown Plymouth, and she'd reconnected with her long-lost sister. The house had been left to her by her best friend and a fellow artist, Rose Dore, who had been murdered in that house by an obsessed admirer.

Her sister Emily, several years her junior, had escaped from the confines of a religious cult in Northern California. Over time, fueled by her own unrelenting determination and aided by the kindness of strangers, she'd finally managed to locate her older sister. For most of her life this missing older sister had been nothing but a vague memory, sustained by the crumpled note she'd found in her apron pocket the morning after "Obedient Charity," which had been Viridienne's name then, disappeared from the compound. That morning, when the truth became known, the escapee's name was removed from all existing records, and she was never spoken of again. But Emily, a little girl of barely seven, knew her sister was real. It kept her going in the dark days and gave her courage to make her own break almost fifteen years later. Now the two women were sitting across from one another at the kitchen table, drinking coffee.

In some ways they would be catching up on what they'd missed for the rest of their lives, but this morning they were simply enjoying breakfast when the house phone rang.

"I'll get it, Em," said Viridienne. She pushed back from the table and reached for the phone on the kitchen counter. "Let's hope it's a potential guest. We could use one."

"Good morning, La Vie en Rose Bed and Breakfast, Plymouth. This is Viridienne Greene speaking."

Within a few moments she flashed a big smile and waved a thumbs-up at her sister. After a concentrated listen she said, "Yes, Mr. Daly, we would consider an extended rental, and yes, we do have a room available. It's a nice big corner one on the first floor. And yes one more time, you can indeed come over this afternoon and take a look. If you like what you see, we can discuss the terms in front of the fire and around a pot of tea."

After she'd arranged a meeting time with the caller, a man named Kevin Daly, and given him a street address, she noted it on the daily business calendar and returned to the table.

"A paying customer?" asked Emily.

"Sounds like a distinct possibility. We'll know more when he comes over this afternoon. He asked if I would do a three-month rental starting on January first, and could he have a monthly rate instead of a weekly or daily rate."

"What did you tell him?' Emily topped up her coffee. She'd only been recently introduced to coffee, and from the look of things she couldn't get enough of it.

"I told him we'd talk about it after he had a chance to look at the room."

"We should probably ask for references for a long-term rental like that. I mean, a man we don't know could end up living with us for three months. What if he snores or leaves the toilet seat up or eats us out of house and home? What if he lets the cat out?"

Viridienne gave her sister a quizzical look. "Look, we're both pretty new at this B&B thing, but we're not stupid. The summer went okay, didn't it? I mean, only one person stiffed us, and she turned out to be a drunk. I counted getting her out of here before she wrecked something a bonus. The loss of room rent was nothing compared to what she could have done."

Emily nodded. "Smoking in bed … and that was just the beginning."

"Don't remind me. And it wasn't just cigarettes. I think she wanted to set up shop here." Viridienne shuddered at the memory and then giggled. "We're going to have to write a book about all of this someday, you know."

"Ya think?"

"I do think. We'd have to change the names, though."

The two were interrupted by the musical ring-tone on Viridienne's cell phone. She pulled it out of her pocket, looked at the ID and smiled, "Hi, Fitz, what's up?"

"I wondered if you two were going to be free this evening. It's my birthday today, and I thought I'd like to celebrate by taking a well-earned break from my current criminal investigation for a little personal indulgence. Pursuant to that thought, I am inviting not one but two lovely women to join me in a celebratory dinner. Tonight."

Viridienne rolled her eyes. "Kissed the Blarney Stone again, have you, my friend?"

"It's all a matter of perspective, and you of all people, artist that you are, ought to know about perspective. So, are you, or you both, available?"

"I know I am. What about you, Em? You up for dinner with an Irish cop tonight? It's his birthday, and it looks like we're the ones getting the presents."

Emily smiled and nodded in the enthusiastic affirmative. She never said no to anything related to food. Cooking was not her forte, but eating most certainly was.

"She says yes. What time?"

After they'd determined the time Detective Inspector Patrick Fitzpatrick would pick them up, Viridienne rang off and gave her sister another thumbs-up, but Emily looked doubtful.

"Are you sure you want your kid sister going out with you on a special date? Don't you want to be alone with him?"

"Look, Em, as far as I'm concerned, we're a package deal. *Mi hermana, su hermana.* I spent a long time worrying about you, not even knowing if you were still alive. If Fitz and I need alone time, you'll be the first to know. Okay?"

"Okay." She cocked her head to one side and looked at her sister. "I can't believe you're dating the detective who solved the murder case of the woman who owned this house."

Viridienne shrugged. "Hunting down criminals is what he does for a living, Em. He's working on another one right now, the man who was found in the water off South Point a couple of weeks back." She shuddered involuntarily. "That was creepy. The papers were all over it when it happened. They said it was a targeted killing, but not much more after that. He can't really talk about it, not that I really want to. But back to your question. I'm not sure if, at my age, it's called dating. We are certainly keeping company, and I really like being with him, and there's absolutely nobody else, but that's as far as it goes. You and I both know what growing up in the Society of Obedient Believers does to a person's attitude towards sex and intimacy. If you're not fighting off an elder with wandering hands, you are bound and beholden to whoever they decide to marry you off to, no questions allowed."

She shuddered at the memory of it and then continued. "I don't mind telling you, it's done a number on me in that department, but Fitz has never once pushed me on the issue. On the other hand, he's super Irish Catholic, and from what he tells me about his own upbringing, it's pretty much as repressive as what we went through. We've been this close," she held up two fingers inches apart, "but no cigar."

Em's eyes went all big. "You mean, you've never …?"

Viridienne, her cheeks quite pink, chewed on her lip and shook her head. "Nope."

"Well, that makes two of us. I managed to get out of the Society in one piece, and for now anyway, I'm leaving it at that. I have absolutely no interest in dating or whatever you want to call it. I have no interest in having a relationship with anyone or doing anything more than working, taking more computer classes and going out with the girls for a glass of wine after work now and then. End of story." Emily held up her mug for emphasis. "Wine and coffee, my new best friends. Now I know why they were forbidden to us growing up. Anything that is fun or good is off limits. Well, I'm good and done with that."

Viridienne looked at her sister across the table and saw a fragile and still very vulnerable woman. This would take time … for both of them.

3

At exactly two in the afternoon the doorbell rang, and Viridienne opened the door to a middling height, middling aged and middling sized man wearing a tweed sports jacket, a navy blue turtle neck and spotless jeans.

"Viridienne Greene?"

She smiled at the man standing in front of her. "Kevin Daly?"

The man on the porch lifted an imaginary hat and said, "I am that very person and not just a cheap imitation, Madame. I am the real deal."

Viridienne chuckled. A little humor was always good way to begin. "Do please come in, and I'll let you have a look at the room. Then, if it's what you are looking for, we can discuss the arrangements over a cup of something hot. Oh, and this is my sister Emily. She lives here with me."

Kevin once again touched the brim of his imaginary hat, nodded in Emily's direction, and stepped over the threshold.

"You said you were interested in a three-month stay. If you like what you see, and we can agree to a rental fee, and considering it's our slow season, you can have your choice of the two rooms on the first floor. We'll also give you exclusive use of the bathroom down here for as long as you stay."

"That's kind of you."

"Do come in and sit down by the fire and let me tell you a little about the house before we start looking at rooms."

"Sounds like a plan," said Kevin.

When the three were seated in the more informal sitting room, Viridienne began her well-practiced introduction to her home and her place of business. Just so much and no more. Not everything. No need to scare the man off by telling him the previous owner had been murdered upstairs. If he was interested, he could read about it in old copies of *The Boston Globe* and the *Old Colony Memorial.*

She sat up a little straighter for emphasis and to command attention and began.

"The house was built in the early 1800s by a Plymouth whaling captain. It was a grand house in its day, and it still is. Of course, we've added indoor plumbing and a new roof, brought in a gas line for the stove in the kitchen, blocked off all of the fireplaces except this one, and added central heat."

"That's reassuring," said Daly with a light chuckle.

"When it came into my hands, I soon realized I didn't need this much house, but if I opened a B&B, I could share its beauty and its history and all this space with whomever walked through the door. So far, so good."

"It's a beautiful place," said Kevin. "I can see why you are so proud of its history."

"So when I decided to make it into a B&B, I got the idea of naming each room for a Mayflower settler, and I decorate each room with Plymouth antiques, when I can find them." She paused and looked around the room with evident pride. "That, I can tell you, is a work in progress, and it's going to take me the rest of my life to finish."

Daly glanced down at his watch. "If you don't mind, Viridienne, and I certainly hope you don't think I'm being rude, but as interesting as this is, I wonder if I can have a rain check on the history, and you could show me the room. I neglected to tell you my time is a bit limited today."

Viridienne almost leapt out of her chair. "Sorry, I get carried away. Of course. Come this way."

Viridienne and Emily, followed by Kevin, turned left and entered the Fuller Room. It was a large west-facing room with a three-window bay that overlooked the front porch and the street in front of the house. It offered a queen-sized bed, an antique carved desk and chair, and two more upholstered chairs for guests. At that time of day, the low sun flooded the room and cast a golden glow on the carpet and furnishings.

"I think this is the nicest room in the house," said Viridienne. "It's light and bright and good for bird- and people-watching, if you are so inclined."

Kevin didn't waste any time. After a fast once-over he said, "Might we look at the other one you mentioned? I think I'd prefer something a little quieter. I'm not so sure about a room in the front. People coming and going and all that. Cars going by. Noise. I'm a quiet man, and I tend to like my privacy."

The second room, The Bradford room, was a little smaller and faced the northeast. It would catch the morning sun, and it would also fall victim to a cruel wind off the ocean in a winter storm. Both rooms had fireplaces, but Viridienne had closed them off. Like the other room, it had a high molded ceiling, softly patterned light toned wallpaper and dark polished woodwork.

"Do these drapes pull shut?" He pointed to the heavy maroon hangings on either side of the window.

"Absolutely. Good idea in a winter storm. It's an old house, and I have double glazed windows throughout, but a northeast wind can get through anything, if it wants to. All you have to do is release the cord on either side. See?" She walked over to the window and demonstrated how it worked.

He nodded in approval. "This room would definitely be quieter. No street noise." He went over to the window and ran his hand along the textured fabric and fingered the heavy cord. "Nice fabric. Thick, too. No one's going to see through that."

"I suppose I never thought of that, but of course you're right. This is a big house and this room is at the very back. The only thing you might hear is a squirrel raiding the bird feeder or the neighborhood raccoon. Otherwise it's quiet as a tomb, especially if you pull those drapes."

"If the choice is mine, then I'll have this one, if you're renting it? Three months and a possible option to extend for another month?"

Viridienne blinked. She hadn't considered that possibility. Extending? "Well, then, let's go into the sitting room and have that coffee or tea I mentioned earlier. I think it's so much easier to talk business over food and drink. Don't you agree, Mr. Daly?"

There really wasn't any other response to make than, "Yes, of course, what a good idea," to which he then added,

"And if we're going to be housemates, do please call me Kevin."

We haven't decided on that yet, my friend, thought Viri-dienne. Let's see how you make it through a cup of coffee and my list of questions.

4

As it turned out, Kevin Daly had all the right answers, and with some hasty coaching earlier in the day from a fellow B&B owner who lived a few miles south of there, Viridienne had all the right questions. Kevin would be happy to provide references; how many did she want? He was fine with renting just the room, and with the addition of a microwave and a coffee maker in the room and a shelf of his own in the fridge in the kitchen, would take care of his own meals. "I have an odd schedule," he said, "and I'd just as soon live on my own time."

"Works for me," said Viridienne. "Now, then, if you are okay with the monthly rate, and you agree to provide me with a month's rent and security deposit in advance, all that remains is for me to think it over one more time and check your references. I'll let you know within the week, and you can come back to sign a letter of agreement. One last question: We have a cat, Old Deuteronomy. We call him DT. I'm surprised he's not here checking you out. I hope you're not allergic."

He smiled and held up both hands. "We always had at least two cats when I was growing up. I love them and would consider DT an added benefit." He paused and looked directly at her, "I'd like to stay here, Viridienne. I hope I pass muster. There's a nice feel to the place. I'm as quiet as a mouse, I promise you." He turned and shook his finger at the cat who had just entered the kitchen.

"Not your kind of mouse, big fella, so watch it." He chuckled at his little joke. "But as I was saying, I keep odd hours. Mostly I telecommute except when I have to visit a job site. So I'll be working away on my own back there, and I promise you'll never hear a peep out of me. In fact, do please let me know if you can hear the radio or the TV. I really don't want to be a bother."

"What you do for work?" asked Emily.

"Independent research consultant, so I'm really self-employed. That's why I'm on the move all the time. People hire me to come into an area and check something out for them. I do the job, they pay me, and I'm off to the next one. I guess I'm kind of a gypsy, but it suits me."

"Interesting," said Viridienne.

Kevin stood and held out his hand. "So, Ms. Maybe-Future-Landlady, I hope I'll be hearing from you before long."

Viridienne and Emily saw him to the door and watched him get into a late model black something-or-other. Viridienne never was good at vehicle identification.

"So what do you think, Em? Shall we, or shall we not?"

"You asked him some pretty good questions, and it would certainly appear that he had the right answers. When did you learn so much about this kind of thing?"

Viridienne went back into the sitting room to gather up the cups. "I confess, I had help. I called Fitz back and asked what he thought. Then I called my friend Evelyn High-tower, the woman who runs the Muted Swan on the other side of town, and picked her brain. She's the one who gave me the list of questions to ask and told me how to ask them."

"What did she tell you to do?"

"Exactly what I did. Sit down in a casual atmosphere. Serve something to eat and drink, ask all the right questions, agree on a price, put it in writing, and while you're at it watch every move he makes. Evelyn even emailed me copies of the rental forms she uses. She told me to sleep on it for at least two days before I make a final decision. She said I could call her if I had any further questions or concerns. Oh, yes, and she told me to make sure I took his picture in case I wanted to do an image search." She made a face. "I forgot to do that."

Emily cocked her head and looked at her older sister, "There's always next time. So, first impression? Yea? Nay?"

"He's a smooth talker, but if he's working with people, he has to be. Clean, good vocabulary, nonsmoker, quiet. If he likes his privacy, he's not going to be bugging us, is he? And he likes cats. That counts double."

"I guess, in the long run, we won't really know until we've lived with him for a while. I will say I made it clear that the rental arrangement would be month to month. It could be that he might not like living with us. That way, we both have an out, if we need it. But I'm going to do as I was told. I'm going to sleep on it for a day or two. Then, if he does move in, and there is a problem, there's always Fitz."

"I don't think I understand," said her sister.

"I didn't bother telling Mr. Daly that I was very good friends with a tough Irish cop named Patrick Fitzpatrick who writes poetry in his spare time."

"You never told me he wrote poetry."

"You never asked," said Viridienne, "and will you look who's just rounded the corner with a fuzzy face full of dead mouse. Hello, DT, whatcha got for me this time?"

Emily wrinkled her nose. "Ugh. Do you think it's a gift or an omen?"

She shrugged her shoulders. "No clue. This is when I wish cats could talk. Meanwhile, if you'll hold the door, I'll escort him and his little snack out onto the screened porch."

5

Hello there, *BIG BOY.* So, you say you're looking for a cuddly teddy bear to drag into your den for long winter nights. I'm a loveable, discreet teddy bear looking for a man who wants to join me on a teddy bear picnic for two. I'll bring the champagne. If you are interested, I can make it happen. Contact me, @TEDDYB, via the site portal.

6

In a back office on the second floor of the Plymouth Police Department Headquarters, Detectives Fitzpatrick and Grey were working on the David Nevins case. They were doing facial recognition searches, comparing the faces of recently murdered gay men around the country and comparing them with images on Facebook and assorted gay men's dating sites. Their progress was maddeningly slow, but at present, it was at least a place to begin. Actually, it was only place they could begin. They had little to nothing else to go on.

The pattern that had emerged so far was that over the last three years, in seemingly random locations, a cluster of three murders of the same description took place within a couple of weeks of one another, and then the killing stopped. But it was always three. The murders were investigated but never solved.

Several months later the pattern of three would be repeated in another part of the country. The murders were identical in description. The victim was garroted shortly after having had sex and left, usually in a back alley or under a bridge or in one of those dark places that foolhardy gay men frequent for a quick nameless and faceless encounter.

This one was different in one respect. The body of the man discovered off South Point had not been left where he'd been murdered, it had been moved. Was there anyone who witnessed the attack? Was there anyone who saw a man stop a car, pull something human sized out, drag it to the edge of the bluff and heave it off, letting it fall onto the rocks and the incoming tide? And if there was such a person, would he or she know what they were witnessing? Newly dead people are floppy. They offer no resistance and for that reason are very hard to transport or move. Fitz and Alison had their work cut out for them. *Merry Christmas.*

7

V iridienne Greene's cat DT for short was a one-eyed orange Maine-coon rescue that tipped the scales at twenty-two pounds and counting. She'd spotted him minutes before he was due to be put down, fallen instantly in love, and they'd been inseparable ever since. He was an excellent judge of character. Viridienne found it surprising that he hadn't come in to check out Kevin Daly, but she reasoned it was because he was busy mousing and oblivious to everything else. Cats were like that, single-minded. But it was hardly a concern, and besides, she had work to do in the studio before going out that evening.

Viridienne was a fiber artist. She was a weaver and a knitter, and she created sculptural fabric collages that weren't exactly quilts but weren't exactly anything else either. Most were commissioned and intended as wall hangings in large open spaces. Because these pieces defied ordinary description, they were loosely categorized as art-quilts or mixed media wall hangings. To make them, she collected odd-bits of yarn and fabric from charity shops, second hand stores and yard sales, and in the privacy of her studio, she worked her magic and turned other people's cast-offs into creative and compelling works of art. In her spare time, she knitted. Useful things like hats and scarves for gifts and for charity, and more organic sculptural creations that looked like shawls, but were more free-flowing in nature. These she displayed, and sometimes even sold, as wearable art. Fiber arts were not big sellers in the art market, but an artist must make art, and selling your creations is a bonus.

For groceries, gas and pocket money, she taught fiber arts at a nearby community college and at the local art center. She also designed and knitted specialty, one-of-a-kind scarves and shawls that she sold out of a local artisan shop, and because of a beloved benefactor, she owned and operated her B&B. All in all, after a rigid and restricted childhood in a religious cult and a daring escape to freedom years earlier, she'd say life was pretty good right now. The jewel in the crown was finding and reuniting with her younger sister. But she took none of it for granted.

The popular New England Biblical admonition that, "pride goeth before a fall," hovered in the corners of her thinking. If she became too self-satisfied, too full of her own success, something bad would happen, but that was an old wives' tale, and she knew it, so she brushed it away. This feeling of accomplishment wasn't pride; it was gratitude. Enough of this mental meandering, she scolded herself. Get your behind in gear and fill those orders.

Fitz showed up exactly when he said he would, six o'clock sharp, dressed for a chilly early December evening out on the town. He was wearing a thick Irish sweater, knit by his grandmother, a tweed flat cap, and topped it all with a triple wrap wool muffler.

She did not tell him he looked like a knitted leprechaun toy standing there on the porch. That would have been rude. But he did. She swallowed the thought and the giggle that went with along it. It didn't help the image with him being a good six inches shorter in height than her own six feet, but early on they'd realized that neither of them fit into the molds that society might have made for them and got on with making the best of what genetics had endowed them with. She was tall and gangly, walked like a great blue heron, had a silver, half-inch buzz haircut, and wore earrings that reached her shoulders. In cold weather she wore a signature ankle-length hand-woven cape. They made quite a pair, and they were enjoying every minute of it.

"Are you ready then, woman?"

"Almost. Come on in and sit for a minute. Em is still getting ready, and I have a couple of questions I want to ask you."

Without asking where they might be sitting, Fitz headed straight for the kitchen, pulled out a chair and sat. He was a kitchen table man. Living rooms and sitting rooms were for Sundays and formal entertaining, visiting clergy and Irish wakes. The kitchen was the heart of the home, the place where you ate, drank, did your homework, gave and received comfort and learned to keep the family secrets.

DT, hearing a familiar voice, wasted no time in setting up a thunderous purr and spreading himself out at the man's feet.

"So where are you keeping all these questions you have for me?" Fitz reached down and gave the cat a thorough rubbing under his chin and behind his enormous ears.

Viridienne made a face. "I suppose they're questions about having a long-term male renter in the house."

"Oh, so he came by, then, did he? And what did you think?"

Viridienne rubbed her chin while she considered her answer. "He seemed fine. He can give us references and a security deposit, said he was quiet and would see to his own meals. I even offered him the use of the back door so he could come and go as he pleased without ever disturbing us or other guests that we hopefully will have."

"So what's the hesitation? I can see it your face. I am a detective in my spare time, you know. I don't just play one on the television." He grinned and waved at her across the table.

"It was nothing he said or did. He was really quite affable. I think it's maybe the idea of having a man I don't really know living in my house for three months."

"You could tell him no. Tell him you thought about it, and for that very reason have changed your mind. No harm in that. You haven't signed anything, have you?"

She shook her head. "No. The thing is, I think it's a piece of my past that's getting to me. You know, men are not nice, not to be trusted, all that crap. It's still getting in the way of things."

"I know it better than you think I do, and I'm still standing here knocking at your door."

She reached across the table and took his hand. "Oh, Fitz, I do trust you. You must know that by now. And it's a lot more than that too. But this is different. This is business, and we need the money. We have no housing expenses to speak of, that's covered in the trust, but we still need to eat, I need to get my art supplies, and Em is going to school. If this is a B&B, a public place of lodging operated for profit, then I can't very well be unwilling to rent to strangers. Just about everyone who walks through my front door is a stranger, present company excepted."

Fitz pondered all of this for a moment before saying, "Basically, you liked the guy, yes? Nothing jumped out at you or Em?"

She nodded.

"Okay, here's what I suggest. Get his references, and I'll go over them with you. We'll check the references up, down and sideways. I'll even run a background check on him at headquarters, and then we tell him the truth."

"What's that?"

"You tell him you've never done a long-term rental before, and you will start with a two-week trial period at the reduced monthly rate you offered him, and then if it doesn't work out on either side, you give him the elbow. It's not like the man is without funds or resources. Besides, it's not really your concern. This is a contractual arrangement, nothing more. It either works, or it doesn't. You live in this place. It's your registered domicile. You can throw out anyone you want at any time, and if he gives you one ounce of trouble, remember, you have me on speed-dial. If you want, I can even make a guest appearance on the day he moves in, should you decide to let him."

"Well, this looks pretty intense," said Emily as she entered the room. "What are you two discussing, the national debt? The nuclear power plant? World peace or the lack thereof? I don't know about you, but I'm starving. Where are we going for dinner?" She paused and flashed Fitz a genuinely radiant smile, "And thank you, Detective, for inviting me along. My sister and I are not joined at the hip. We're not a package deal."

Any further discussion of long-term renters or the national debt was temporarily kitchen tabled in favor of dinner. Fitz stood and held out his two elbows to the women standing on either side of him.

"My goodness, is this *two* much of a good thing? I think I feel a poem coming on."

"Uh oh."

"Roses are red, and violets blue, one lady's good, but better is two."

"I'll go get my cape while you apologize for that," said Viridienne.

OVER A CONVIVIAL DINNER at The Warbling Oyster, a new restaurant on the waterfront, the three went over the pros and cons of having a long-term resident and in the end decided that Fitz's plan was likely the best. Do a two-week trial run and make a final decision after that.

"It's possible that he might not like those terms, you know." Fitz was doing full justice to an after-dinner Irish coffee and a great slab of birthday cake Viridienne had secretly requested as they came in. "He might just decide to chuck the whole thing and look elsewhere."

"I just need to get past this personal stuff," said Viridienne. "I have you to call if I need it. We can lock off the upstairs part of the house where we live from the downstairs rooms. We had absolutely no problems this summer." She was gesticulating with her fork, and Fitz was staying well out of range. Viridienne had very long arms.

"And ..."

"And if the references check out, I'm going to say yes."

"Now then." Fitz put down his fork, dabbed and at his mouth with his linen napkin. "I don't know about you two, but I think a perfect end to this evening would be to go off and find us a Christmas tree for your first Christmas in the new house."

If Viridienne noticed he was making greater and greater use of the first person plural, she made no mention of it, but neither did she correct him.

"I've never had a Christmas tree," said Em.

Fitz put down his napkin and pushed back from the table. "Well, we'll soon put an end to that, then, won't we, Woman?"

8

The Christmas tree hunt was a resounding success. Em was like a little kid in a candy store; she wanted everything she saw. Viridienne was only marginally more subdued, but she too was happier than she ever remembered. She was having honest-to-goodness, genuine fun.

In the past she'd pretty much ignored Christmas. It only brought back memories of what she'd missed in her growing up years. Sometimes she and Rose, the woman whose house she now owned and inhabited, would treat themselves to what some people referred to as a Jewish Christmas: Chinese food and a movie on December 25th. They had no family to visit or ignore. This was different.

They finally settled on a positively enormous tree, one that would take up a good portion of Viridienne's sitting room and reach all the way up to the ten-foot ceiling—after trimming back the top. On top of that, because the man selling the Christmas trees recognized Fitz as being one of "Plymouth's finest," the tree was a gift.

"Keeping company with a man of the law has its bene-fits," said Fitz on the drive home. The tree was well roped on the roof, the top flopping in front of the windshield and the far end sticking out past the tail pipe and adorned with a red bandana. Many of the houses they passed were already decorated for the holiday, and by the time the three got back to the house, they were more than ready to deck the halls. However, getting the thing through the door proved to be more of a challenge than any of them might have anticipated. In the end they had to settle for standing it in a bucket of water on the front porch until such time as they worked out the logistics and moved some furniture in preparation for the formal installation. It was only then, standing there with her sister and Fitz, that Viridienne remembered she had neither a Christmas tree stand nor ornaments and not much of a budget for either.

"It's too late for solving problems of that nature, Viridi-enne. Let's go inside and have a drink of something cold or hot or in between. I've had all the excitement I can stand for one day, being my birthday and all, and I'm ready to sign off. With your permission, we can take all of this up tomorrow. For now all I can say is, I've had some experi-ence in the Christmas tree department." He held up his index finger. "You have a tree. I have a plan."

Inside the spacious and comfortable kitchen, the three sat around the table drinking mugs of hot chocolate topped with whipped cream. DT had come running when he heard the sound of the squirt-can and demanded his own serving, which he was now noisily enjoying under the table.

Viridienne excused herself for a moment and returned carrying an exceptionally poorly wrapped package which she set on the table in front of Fitz.

"For me?" He clapped his free hand to his chest.

"I do believe you are the only person of the male persuasion having a birthday in this room. Yes, for you, silly man."

Fitz pulled apart the wrappings and lifted out a long, beautifully patterned blue cashmere scarf. "You made this, didn't you?"

Viridienne smiled. "I did. And I made it long enough to loop around your neck twice and still be long enough to keep your belly warm. Happy Birthday to you, my very special friend."

Fitz stood, wrapped the scarf around his neck, and holding the two ends in each hand, reached up and both hugged and wrapped Viridienne into the rest of it.

"Thank you, my love," he whispered.

And then the phone rang.

"I'll get it," said Em, scrambling for the house phone.

"Let the answering machine take it," said Viridienne, untangling herself from scarf and Fitz. "There's nothing that can't wait until morning."

"You've reached La Vie en Rose Bed and Breakfast. We are not at the desk right now, but if you will leave your name and number and a brief message, we will get back to you as soon as we can."

"Viridienne, this is Kevin Daly. I know I first talked about coming in January, but some things have changed. If you find my references acceptable and you still are considering me as a long-term rental, I wonder if we might talk about my moving in sooner. Possibly next week? Something's come up business-wise, and it would be better for me if I had a home base. Nicer, too. I understand if you can't, and I'm certainly not homeless, but hotels and motels are so plastic and impersonal this time of year. My call back number is the same as it was the other day, but I'll leave it anyway. I hope you and your sister are having a pleasant evening."

"I'll call him in the morning," said Viridienne.

"First thoughts?" asked Fitz

Viridienne wrinkled her nose in consternation. "I'd actually decided to say yes, if the references check out. But that was yes to him arriving in January. I think I wanted to have Christmas by myself…well, with you two. I'm not sure I want anyone else here."

"You can always say no. You don't need a reason. This is your home; you live here, and you are the boss."

She nodded. "You're right, but I hate to think of him spending Christmas in a motel. I never cared about Christmas." She paused and looked at the man sitting across the table. "Now maybe I'm beginning to."

"Fair enough. Sleep on it. And while we're still on the subject, what, may I ask, might you and your lovely little sister be doing for Christmas? I know where you'll be, but I'm wondering how you'll be doing it?"

She shrugged. "Good question, and I have no idea. I do, however, have a good friend with whom I might be able to consult on the matter of holidays?"

Fitz bowed low, "At your service anytime, Lady Greensleeves."

Viridienne, looking perplexed, held up her arms. "I'm not wearing green."

"Greensleeves is the title of an old English and Irish Folk song. Your name, is actually Green Greene, isn't it?"

She nodded. "I didn't think too many people would catch on to that. It's my own little in-joke with myself."

Fitz held up an expository finger. "I looked it up." He leaned back in his chair and began to sing. "Alas, my love, you do me wrong, to cast me out discourteously. And I have loved you oh so long, delighting in your company."

"On top of everything else, you're an Irish tenor?"

"So I've been told. But for God's sake don't tell anyone. It's bad enough that I write poetry. I'll never live it down at the stationhouse."

"Who would I tell?"

"Alison."

"I thought she knew everything there was to know about you."

He touched the side of his nose with his index finger. "There are some things a man doesn't want advertised. Let's just leave it at that, my dear. Promise me that, and I'll sing to you again sometime."

She touched her fingers to her forehead in a mock salute.

9

The next day Viridienne was still stewing over whether to let Kevin Daly move before the first of the year. Wasn't Christmas a family time? On the other hand, her total family consisted of her sister and herself, and if she stretched it, Fitz, by invitation. Truth be told, she was looking forward to having a real Christmas, whatever that meant. It would be her first since her parents took themselves and their daughter out of the secular world and became life-long and fully committed members of the Society of Obedient Believers. Could she do that with a renter living there? What would be her obligation to him? Fitz was right, she could just say no. But did she want to?

"Have you started checking his references yet?" Emily bounced into the kitchen. She was a cheery, chatty early bird in full feather. "Is the coffee still hot? I think DT is at the door with another tasty morsel for us, but I didn't let him in."

"It's on today's to-do list—that and a lot of other things,

including delivering an order for the Christmas shop at the art center."

"Is it more of those lacy scarves and shawls you've been making? They're flying out of there. They are really beautiful. I'm amazed at all the things you can do." Em was filling a massive mug of coffee for herself.

Viridienne nodded and pointed to herself. "I'm amazed the art thing is still in there after all those years with the Believers. Did I ever tell you what happened when they discovered my secret stash of yarn scraps and fabric cuttings? I was around twelve, I think. I'd been sneaking them out of the sewing room when I thought no one was looking. Then, if I finished my work early, I'd hide myself away and make things out of my scraps. The world I lived in was pretty bleak back then, but at least I could run away to my pretty bits. Even then I craved color and texture. Somebody must have seen what I was doing and told one of the elders. They caught me one day and burned everything up right there in front of me and then shunned me for a whole month. It was awful. They treated me like I was dead. Even our own parents shunned me."

Em shook her head. "And those parents are still out there, happy as pigs in shit! I wonder if they ever think about us."

"We both know they're not supposed to, and it's best not to dwell on it. To be honest, when I broke out, I never gave them another thought. They made their choice, and the day I turned eighteen I made mine. I missed having parents, but not them." She paused, her voice cracking. "The only thing I held out hope for was finding you."

"And here I am, the geeky little sister; business partner, keeper of the books and the keys, dishwasher-in-chief, and I can't boil water unless I have a recipe. You're the gourmet cook, artsy one, I'm the practical one, and together we've got this thing covered!" Emily raised her mug and saluted her sister and continued her stream of consciousness.

"Hey, I've got an idea. You drop off the stuff for the artisan shop, and I'll make a hit-and-run raid on the supermarket for milk, coffee and cat food. When I get back, I'll make the reference calls, and I'll even do an internet search. If there's anything we need to know about Mr. Kevin Daly, trust me, I'll find it. Then we can talk it over one more time while we have lunch. Deal?"

Viridienne grinned, taking pleasure in her sister's boundless enthusiasm. She was slower and more deliberative by nature. "Twist my arm. You know I hate anything to do with administrative work. I'll even make us lunch." She was already up, and on her way out of the kitchen.

While Viridienne was dropping off the completed order at the Artisan Shop, and Emily was making the grocery run, Kevin Daly called and left a message on the house phone.

"Viridienne, its Kevin Daly. I was thinking. When I told you I wanted to move in early, what I really meant to say was, I am in need of a place to park my clothes and things while I make my local business contacts and arrangements. I already have plans for Christmas, so I wouldn't be under your feet for the holidays. At the most I'd only be staying there for a couple of nights from the time when I drop off my stuff until the beginning of the New Year when I would begin my official tenancy—if you accept me, that is. I would of course pay the full amount of rent for the convenience. Call and let me know when you've decided. Thank you."

Over a lunch of vegetable soup and open-faced broiled cheddar-on-rye bread sandwiches, Viridienne and Emily listened for a second time to the message on the machine and then agreed they would rent a room to Kevin Daly for three months, and they would give him permission to come in early to drop off his things.

"Do you think we could check with Fitz before we call Kevin?" Em was making short work of her soup and sandwich and clearly relishing every morsel. Food in the compound was basic fodder. It sustained you. You weren't supposed to relish it. All of your energy and all of your senses were to be directed to God. Anything else was considered work of the devil. Life was grey, food was bland, no music—not even hymns—and absolutely no poetry.

"Viridienne? You in there? I just asked you a question."

"Mmmph? Oh dear. Sorry, I was a million miles away."

"By the look of you, it wasn't a very nice trip."

"Right in one, sister. But I did hear your question, and I don't think we need to bother Fitz. He's got enough to do, driving around in that black and white panda-car of his, enforcing the law and chasing down bad guys."

"And women," added Em. "There are bad women out there, too."

"More of them are men. But enough of that. I think we can handle this on our own. So tell me, what did you turn up in the reference check while I was out? Any red flags?"

"Just the opposite. If there ever was a perfect tenant, it's Kevin Daly. Two previous landlords said he was quiet, neat, and paid the rent on time, and the room was spotless when he moved out. Anything I could find on Google and LinkedIn backed up what he said he did for work. Also, nothing at all on the criminal record background site. He's either squeaky clean, or he's the world's he most meticulous confidence man, but I'm inclined to think he's okay. I think we should rent him a room. If it doesn't work out, blame me, call Policeman Fitz, and we evict him. But I say, let's give it a shot."

Viridienne chewed on her lower lip. "I'm almost there. Give me till supper time."

"What's the problem?"

"It's not him, it's me. I was fine with him moving in in January, pending the reference check, of course. I think his wanting to move the date forward a couple of weeks threw me a curve. You know me, I need to think things over. I don't like surprises. Give me a little time, and I'll be fine. We'll call him with a yea or a nay right after supper. Promise."

That evening Viridienne sent a text message to her soon-to-be-tenant.

"Hi, Kevin. It's Viridienne Greene. I discussed your request with my sister, and we agreed that it's okay if you move in early next week. Give me a call tomorrow morning, and we can go over the how and when of it, and I can give you keys to both the front and back doors."

It took less than a minute for Viridienne's phone to sound the response: "Thank you, Viridienne, this means a lot to me. I will call you in the morning."

Viridienne had no sooner disconnected when the phone rang again. This time it was Fitz, saying he'd managed to come up with a box or two of Christmas decorations, and if they were going to be home, was it okay if he brought them over in an hour or so?

"I don't have to ask who that was," said Em with an impish grin on her face.

"That obvious, is it?"

She nodded. "The goofy grin on your face says it all."

∾

Greensleeves was my delight,
Greensleeves my heart of gold
Greensleeves was my heart of joy
And who but my lady Greensleeves.

I have been ready at your hand
To grant whatever thou would'st crave;
I have waged both life and land
Your love and goodwill for to have.

Greensleeves was my delight,
Greensleeves my heart of gold
Greensleeves was my heart of joy
And who but my lady Greensleeves.

10

At precisely nine in the morning, Kevin Daly called on the house phone, and Viridienne, pencil and note pad at the ready, picked it up in what served as the business office. Shortly after moving in, she'd partially repurposed an oversized, windowed butler's pantry off the kitchen to serve as a place to keep the business computer and occupancy records and still serve as storage for some of the larger kitchen supplies. Space wise, Fitz would describe it as not being big enough to swing a cat, but it had everything she could possibly need, all within arm's reach. With floor-to-ceiling shelves covering the walls on either side of the door and a window that opened over the kitchen garden providing an abundance of natural light, it was as inviting as it was practical.

In truth, the office was really Emily's domain. She was a quick study and an absolute natural with computers. She'd learned a lot about record keeping when she was still living in the religious compound. Now, always learning as she went along, she became the family business woman and computer geek. She kept meticulous files and records and was now working her way through the legal side of doing business in a small and fiercely historic town. Give her facts and figures and linear predictions, and she was in hog heaven, as she would put it. The two sisters were a perfect balance.

Viridienne was both creative and practical but had a decided aversion to the precision that computers and running a business demanded. She was the artist, the visionary, the inventive cook and the official greeter. Now she was greeting the man who was about to become their first long-term renter.

"Good morning, Kevin. So tell me when you'd like to come over and settle in."

"Well, if it's just the same to you, Viridienne, I'd like to move my things in sometime this week. I've got plans to go see my mother for Christmas, and it would be good to be unpacked and settled and not be packing and unpacking out of suitcases all over again, if you know what I mean."

"I can understand that. The holidays are crazy enough without adding insult to injury. Where does your mother live?"

"She's in a retirement community in southern Maine, in Saco. She grew up there, and she always wanted to go back. It works for her, and it's not too far from Portland airport, if I'm far away, and only about two hours' drive from here. I try and get up there a couple of times a year."

"That's good of you. Not everybody makes the effort these days."

"It's my mother. You only get one."

Viridienne felt her eyes start to prickle. The rush of memories of a mother she hadn't seen for years and a mother who would never make the effort to see her now blindsided her. She squeezed her free hand into a fist and quickly regained control.

"Viridienne? You there? Have we lost the connection?"

"I'm here. A momentary distraction. The cat knocked something over. Sorry about that. How does this coming Thursday afternoon sound to you?"

"It sounds about as good as it can get. How is two in the afternoon? Then I won't be interrupting your lunch or your dinner."

"Great. See you on Thursday then. Meanwhile, give me your email, and I'll send the rental agreement for you to look over one more time."

"Who was that, Vid?" Emily was pouring her second oversized coffee of the morning.

"Our new lodger. It's official. Kevin Daly will be moving his things in this Thursday afternoon—and he's going to be off seeing his mother for Christmas, so we don't have to be concerned about him being alone for the holiday."

"Technically, it's none of our concern if he's alone for the holiday. This is a business arrangement."

"You're right, Em, but we both know we'd be thinking about it, especially if we are doing presents around a fire, and he's here by himself, locked away in his room with a TV dinner. You wouldn't be able to stand that any more than I could. But now we don't have to think about it, and that's good."

"You gonna tell Fitz?"

"I suppose, not that he has anything to do with how we run the B&B. On the other hand, he does seem to have a more than a casual interest in this place."

"Ya think?" Emily grinned at her sister. "I'm going to toast up a bagel, you want one?"

Viridienne shook her head and dropped into a chair at the kitchen table.

"He's a good man, and I have to say I really like having him in my life. It's nice to have someone I can trust and depend on. I wish the same for you, when you're ready."

Emily gave her sister an odd look and shook her head. "I do give that some thought once in a while, but we both know you don't walk out of something like we did and turn into a normal person overnight. I'm still finding out what my normal is." She paused and chewed on her lip. "There's so much I don't know about relationships, any relationships. Look at us. You are my sister, and we're still getting to know each other. I don't even know how to ask the right questions, because I don't know what they are yet." Then she brightened. "Anyway, it's not like I have to make a decision by the end of the week, is it?" She laughed, but it was a high nervous laugh.

"God knows we're both as green as grass in that department, but I'm definitely progressing," Viridienne said reassuringly. She paused, winked and gave her younger sister an odd smile. "This could be an interesting Christmas. I think I might be ready to take the big step."

Emily, now wide-eyed, responded by setting down her coffee bucket and flashing the time-out signal with her two hands. "Too much information, lady, but if you do, just remember to lock your door and hang a Do Not Disturb card on the handle."

This left them both in fits of giggles. It was time to start the day. Em would be giving the soon-to-be occupied back bedroom a good once over before Kevin Daly moved in.

11

Viridienne had a final class to teach at the art center and a flurry of errands to do after that. Fitz was coming over that evening for dinner and to oversee the installation and decoration of the tree. Her very first ever, real Christmas tree.

Is this what normal looks like? Viridienne asked herself as she cleared off the table and set the dishes in the sink. If it is, I think I could get to like it.

FITZ ARRIVED JUST after four-thirty that same afternoon. It was already dark, and a scattering of tiny snowflakes had collected and were glittering on his shoulders as he waited for Viridienne to come to the door. He looked a sight, grinning from ear to ear, a bottle of something in a brown paper bag wedged under an arm, a lumpy trash bag filled with cast-off Christmas ornaments in one hand and a galvanized bucket of rocks swinging from the other.

"Rocks and trash for me? You shouldn't have."

"Shouldn't have what, woman, the rocks or the bottle? You can't put up a Christmas tree without either one of them. It's one of the rules, and in case you hadn't noticed it by now, as an officer of the law it is my bounden duty to observe the law."

Viridienne, laughing, held open the door and looked over the man's shoulder. "How come you have an official vehicle? You don't usually use them. I didn't think it was allowed."

"Long story. Ask the man who rear-ended me. So are you going to let me in sometime today, or are you just going stand there and watch me freeze solid before your very eyes?"

"Get in here, you eejit."

"Ah. I can see my influence is finally beginning to take effect. Eejit! Fine old Irish term of affection, that!" And just to prove his point, he leaned up and kissed her.

Once inside, dusted off and warmed up with a huge cup of strong tea, Fitz, by popular vote, took charge of positioning and setting up the tree. Viridienne quickly learned that according to family tradition, the bucket of rocks would serve as the tree stand. Then, once the tree was firmly wedged into place and staked to triangulating corner window handles, her job would be to keep it watered and clean up after the cat when he began, as he undoubtedly would, to rearrange the ornaments. She could do that.

DT, crouched in his preferred chair, was watching every move. This was totally new to him, but already the creative possibilities were expanding by the minute. If cats could smile, he'd be smiling.

Viridienne learned that setting up a tree, particularly one of the size they had chosen, was no small undertaking. It definitely required a glass of wine, not a few accompanying blows and curses, and a lot of helpless laughter to finally get the damn thing upright and secure. They did eventually succeed and by mutual agreement called out for a pizza for supper. Once fed and watered, they could begin the decoration.

After dinner, and because Viridienne and Em had no history or experience to call upon, Fitz happily agreed to conduct Operation Decoration. He reached into the trash bag and hauled out a tangle of wires and tiny light bulbs.

"First holy mystery: untangle the lights." He handed the spaghetti-like mass to Emily, the methodical sister.

"Second holy mystery: sort and select the ornaments." He pulled out a tatty cardboard box held together with a shoelace and handed it to Viridienne, the color and shape expert.

"And what is the third holy mystery then, Detective?"

"A wee cup of Irish coffee while you two attend to your women's work."

"Chauvinist!" Viridienne fired a crumpled wad of tissue paper at the man and scored a direct hit.

"Felonious slur …"

The sound of the doorbell interrupted their playful exchange.

"You expecting someone? Do you want me to get it?" asked Fitz.

Viridienne shook her head no and then nodded yes.

"No to your first question since I'm not expecting anyone, and yes, please go and see who it is. We don't get door-to-door salesmen any more, just the Latter Day Saints and the Jehovah's Witnesses, so tell them thanks but no thanks."

Emily cocked her head and looked quizzically at her sister. "Who are they?"

Viridienne started to answer when Fitz called out from the front door, "Hey Vid, a Mr. Kevin Daly is asking for you."

"Be right there." Viridienne set the pile of mismatched decorations to one side and went to the door. "Kevin, you told me Thursday, so I wasn't expecting you. I'm sorry, that's not very welcoming, is it? Come in out of the cold."

Fitz stepped back, arms crossed in front of his chest, and Kevin, passing close in front of him, entered the hallway. "I hope I'm not intruding on something, and honestly, I'm not trying to move in early. It's just that I happened to be nearby and wondered if I could drop off a couple of boxes. I probably should have called, but I decided to do a drive by, and if I saw lights, I'd knock on the door and at least ask. Then I saw the police car out front, and I got worried there might be something wrong in here, so I made it my business to stop and check on you two."

Fitz lowered his shoulders and let his arms fall partway to his sides.

"That's really kind of you, Kevin. We're trimming the Christmas tree, and of course you can drop off some boxes." She turned toward the man standing close beside her. "This is Fitz. Detective Fitzpatrick. He's one of Plymouth's finest and a close friend of the family."

After a fractional hesitation Fitz held out his hand, and Kevin shook it.

"Where are the boxes? I'll give you a hand."

"In the back of my car. It's parked behind yours. But the snow's coming down faster now, so I'll do it. You don't have to get cold and wet when I still have my coat on. Besides, it's only two cartons, books and summer clothes."

"No problem. I'll give you a hand, and we'll both be out

of the weather, and you'll be back on your way in half the time."

It was neither a question nor a social nicety. Under the pleasant Irish lilt, there was no mistaking the intent. Detective Fitzpatrick had just hammered his stake into the ground, and he wanted to have a closer look at and inside the man's car.

12

"So that's your long-term renter, is it?" Fitz, according to the first rule of tree decoration, was looping the lights around the tree. Starting at the top, he tossed and draped and snagged the uncooperative string until he'd used up every inch of it.

"What's your first impression of Kevin Daly?" asked Viridienne. She was sitting on the sofa, waiting to start positioning the ornaments.

"He seems okay. If you're asking if any warning bells went off in my head, the answer is no."

"You sure? I mean, you'd tell me if they did, right, because I can't say you looked entirely welcoming when you answered the door."

Fitz's cheeks grew pink. "I was getting all unnecessary, Vid. A stranger came to my lady friend's door, and I snapped into police mode and immediately started checking him out. I'm afraid it comes with the trade."

"And he checked out?"

Fitz nodded. "So far, anyway. But I don't think it did

any harm for him or any other male lodger, for that matter, to know that an officer of the law is in regular attendance here. Think of it as an added security system. *Pro bono*, of course." He winked. "I do have a vested interest in your wellbeing and that of your dear sister."

Viridienne didn't have a response to that, so she let a grateful smile say it all.

"If the lady of the house has no objection, I'll find a way to swing by on Thursday afternoon when he settles in. Nothing wrong with underscoring the point."

"More like marking your territory, Detective."

"And would that be meeting with your approval, Ms. Greene?"

Emily was watching them from her spot in the corner, and she, too, smiled her approval.

"I will take it under consideration, sir. Meanwhile, can we please start arranging the ornaments? I feel like a little kid. I am all excited. I have memories of Christmases before we entered the society, but they're fuzzy. We didn't have much. I remember we had to wait until Christmas Eve to get a tree. That's when they practically gave them away. It was pretty grim. But that was then, and this is now." She stood and went over to the massive tree. "Should I start at the top and work my way down?"

"I don't really have a rule for that. My da did the lights and got drunk. That was his contribution. My mam always did the ornaments, such as they were, and the finished effect was magical. More than magical, when you're a little boy and everything is a wonder."

I wouldn't know, thought Viridienne, but she kept it to herself and pulled a fragile red glass bell out of the box. She held it up for all to see and hung it on the tree.

Emily joined in at once, and the two women, one

methodical and one impetuous, managed to place all the ornaments but the two they broke. Fitz was supervising the operation from the far end of the sofa over his Irish coffee.

"That's it. We've done it." Emily stepped back to survey her handiwork and then asked, "But what about the top. Aren't we supposed to have an angel or a star or something extra special up there?"

"We're going to need a ladder to put anything that high," said Viridienne. "It took every inch of my six feet to reach even near the top. Being tall has its advantages sometimes."

"Being tall is what you are, Viridienne, and you wear it well. I'm sure I'll be asking you to get things down from the top shelves from time to time. Sure beats hauling out a ladder."

"It took me a long time to like it, Fitz. Six feet tall and built more like a stork than a woman, but what the heck, it's me, and I'm good with it. But back to the point, what about the top of the tree?"

Fitz saluted her with his almost empty coffee cup. "I thought about getting something on the way here, an angel or a star or something, but then I thought you might like to pick one out or even make it yourself, considering you're an artist and all that. It's not like I forgot."

Viridienne's mind was already off and away, not with visions of sugar plums but with gold and silvery threads and some unspun wool she'd been saving until she had a reason to do it. Now she did, and it would be her secret until she completed her project. "I have the beginnings of an idea," she said.

"Better fasten your seatbelt, Fitz," said Emily. "I've seen that look on her face before."

"Good heavens, woman. Would you look at the time? I

have to be up bright and early tomorrow, which, considering the time of year, means it will still be dark outside. We might have a serious lead on the murder case we've been working on, and it's all hands on deck. Just the thing for the holidays."

"Are you talking about the man they found off South Point a couple of weeks ago?"

He nodded. "I am, but you know I can't discuss an active case."

Viridienne put a protective hand on his arm. "I know, Fitz, just be careful, okay? I'll walk you to the door."

Fitz wished Emily a good night, and he and Viridienne went out and lingered like a couple of breathless teenagers in the unlighted foyer. It was taking them longer and longer to say goodnight, and while they both knew what the inevitable and eventual outcome to all of this extended foreplay was going to be, they both seemed hesitant about taking it to a higher level of unwedded bliss until that very moment. Viridienne stepped back, keeping her hands resting on Fitz's shoulders.

"You don't always have to leave, you know. I wouldn't mind, one day, if you stayed the night." Viridienne had decided to make the first and fateful move herself, and it stopped him dead in his tracks. When he did manage to recover himself, he spluttered, "Really? Uh, isn't the man supposed to be the one to ask … and what about your sister… and dear God in heaven, woman, whatever will I say to my sainted mother?"

"Let's talk more about this tomorrow. It's all food for thought."

"I'm hungry." Fitz pulled her closer.

"So am I, my friend. It just took me a while to realize it. I'm glad you waited."

The man sitting at the computer logged into his Facebook business account and typed, Geoffrey Hartt wants to be friends with you on Facebook.

I THINK you must have the wrong person; I don't know you.

THIS IS A REAL LONG SHOT, but I think we went to high school together. I hope you don't mind me contacting you. I work for the government, and I'm living out of the country for the next 2 years. It gets lonely, especially since my wife died, and my children are grown and living back in the states. It's just me and the dog here. I'm only looking for a pen pal, and you look familiar. I'm just looking for someone to write to in the long empty hours away from home. I was scrolling around on Facebook, and I came across your picture, and like

I said, I think we went to the same high school, Jersey South in Cherry Hill? Sound familiar? I was a senior, and you were just a sophomore. Anyway, that's for another time, I hope. Can we be FB friends? Just pen-pals. I live too far away to ask you out on a date, but if you are the same girl, I went to high school with, who knows? Maybe we can make it happen. Hahaha!

∼

I DID GO to Jersey South, but I don't remember you. Are you sure it's me?

∼

YOU CAN'T BE sure of anything anymore these days, can you? Good thing to ask. I remember the headmaster/principal was named Dr. Orton, and Miss Sharkey taught Spanish. She was a favorite. Does this sound familiar?

∼

OMG, that's it, all right.

∼

I LIVED ON COMMONWEALTH ROAD…WHERE did you live?

∼

VINAL AVENUE, number 22, but I don't think the house is there any more.

∼

Would you believe I used to walk down that street on the way to school? Of course, those were the days before everyone had cars and kids still knew how to use their legs. Oops, time to get to work. I'll get back to you later today, if it's ok with you.

≈

I guess so.

≈

That's great…you've made my day. Let's make this happen. TTYL

The man at the computer was pleased. It had been a good year for him financially, and if these two new ones stayed on the line along with the others, it would be even better next year. He bookmarked the page and moved on to his next correspondent.

Hi again, I just grabbed a few minutes and thought I'd check in, and see if you are willing to be my pen-pal? There must be a better term for electronic pen pals Maybe we'll find it. "Pen-pal" sounds too much like high school. On the other hand, we de seem to have that in common, don't we? So when you get this, don't keep me in suspense, let me know, okay? Let's make it happen. Hope you are having a good day. Goeff

≈

John Robin has sent you a message.

. . .

Hi, there. This is a real long shot, but I think we went to high school together. I hope you don't mind me contacting you. I work for the government, and I'm living out of the country for the next 2 years. It gets lonely here, especially since my wife died, and my children are grown and living back in the states. It's just me and the dog here. I'm just looking for a pen pal, nothing more, just someone to talk to in these long empty hours away from home. I came across your picture, and like I said, I think we went to the same high school, Santa Anna? It was a small Catholic secondary school outside of San Diego. I was a senior and you were a sophomore, and I have to say you look really familiar. Can we be FB friends and write to each other? I live too far away to ask you out on a date. But pen pals are a safe bet, don't you think? If you are that same girl, then lets' make it happen. Hahaha!

∿

I went to Santa Anna, but I can't say you look familiar.

∿

You can't be sure of anything anymore these days, can you? Of course, I've changed over the years, but if you go on line and look at the year book, you'll find someone that I looked like thirty years ago. Good thing to ask, though, you can't be too careful these days. That's why I suggested looking it up. Do you remember the headmaster, Brother Anthony? He loved music and basketball. Everybody loved him. Does this sound familiar?

∿

I can't believe it; this is so weird. Yes, I did go there.

∿

I LIVED ON FRANKEN CIRCLE, where did you live?

~

Rosaria Lane

~

I CAN'T BELIEVE THIS, I used to walk by that street on the way to school. Of course, those were the days before everyone had cars, and kids still knew how to use their legs. Oops, time to go to work. If it's okay with you, can I get back to you later today? Lets' make this happen.

~

I'LL BE at work this afternoon, but I don't see why not.

~

"ONE MORE," he said aloud to himself. "And then I'll take a break,

So, teddy bear boy, shall we stop all this talk and no action? How about we meet up for a bite to eat and a drink and get to know each other a little better? Don't you think it's about time we should … make things happen?

~

SOUNDS DELICIOUSLY TEMPTING. Where and when do you suggest we meet?

HOW ABOUT TOMORROW night at the *Home Plate* on *River street.* *It's a popular sports bar. Good food, good music, dark corners . After that, maybe we can take a walk around the center of town and look at the Christmas lights. I love Christmas, don't you? Especially the fairy lights.*

AND WHAT HAPPENS AFTER THAT?

LET'S *see how it goes, fuzzy boy. You know what we teddy bears are like, up for anything and into everything just as long as it's warm and furry (he says with a lascivious leer)! I'm an action man. I make things happen.*

14

After Fitz drove off into falling the snow, Viridienne, her face flushed, returned to the living room and curled into her favorite corner of the sofa. The only light in the room was coming from the tree, and the effect was magical. She and her sister, each alone with her thoughts, sat in companionable silence until the silvery crash of a glass ornament hitting the floor followed by the scrabbling sound of DT tearing out of the room brought them back to the present.

"Damned cat!" said Viridienne.

"We knew it was bound to happen. Once burned, once learned? I think he scared the living bejeesus out of himself. Maybe he'll leave it alone after this?"

"I doubt it, he's a cat. That's one of the reasons Fitz staked the tree in two directions. Curiosity is his middle name. He can't help himself. I think to be on the safe side we need to shut him out of the living room when we're both out of the house."

"Good point. I think if I was a cat, I'd do the same

thing." Emily gestured to the twinkling tree. "Meanwhile, better safe than sorry. I've never seen anything so beautiful. I mean, I've seen pictures, and all those years ... well, you know."

"I do know—pretty but not for me. Maybe that's how Jewish people feel at this time of year. Look but don't touch. If I ever get the opportunity, I will ask. There are a couple of Jewish girls in my management class."

Emily nodded. "Meanwhile, what are you going to make for the top of the tree? Any pictures that I've seen always have a star or an angel or even just an extra fancy ornament up there. What are we going to have?"

"Well, I have to admit, ever since Fitz mentioned it, my brain has been at work. But I'm going to surprise you both. Angels and stars don't do it for me. Too many religious overtones."

"But Vid, the whole Christmas thing is all about the birth of Jesus. Even in the Society we observed that much of it."

Viridienne blew out a breath of disgust. "Sure, we did ... extra prayer, extra work duty and even harsher food restrictions to remind us that we were unworthy of so great of gift, and we needed to atone even more than usual. All that for a savior who never showed up. Just wonderful, wasn't it?" She was working herself into a full-fledged rant. "What they didn't tell us is that Jesus was likely born in April, and the early Christians, who were hell bent on converting the country folk, moved his birthday around to fit one of their seasonal rituals. That's what heathen means, you know, people of the heath. Anyway, as the Jesus cult expanded, they positioned the Christian religious festivals to coincide with the pagan seasonal festivals. Christmas lights, Yule logs, celebrating the return of light in the dark of winter. Bunnies and eggs and flowers, signs of spring and symbols of fertility and rebirth. Do you see the connection? Jesus did not walk out of the tomb with an Easter bunny in his arms. Some advertising genius from a chocolate factory put it there! And people wonder why I think religion is a joke. Because it is. It's a convenience, a way to control people's behavior." She paused for breath and with some effort ratcheted herself down a couple of notches.

"Sorry, Em. I just get so mad at what a load of crap we were fed. It's all going to take some getting over, but maybe this will be a beginning. I'm so glad you found me." She stopped again and opened her arms. "And thank you, Rose, for this beautiful house—a place where we can start over." Further words failed as the memory of her beloved, quick-moving, bright-eyed friend washed over her.

Emily got up from her chair and gave her sister a comforting hug. "We'll get there, Vid. We'll get there, and just think, we both have your goodhearted Irish Catholic Fitz to help us along the way." She held up an expository finger to make her point.

"That we do, Em, but he's kind of a mixed blessing."

"Whatever do you mean by that?"

Viridienne paused and considered her words before speaking. "Well, we both know I'm a couple of years older than he is."

"Is that a problem?"

"Not really. He's a very complex man, and he's amazingly understanding and patient with the likes of me, but let's not talk about that now. Whatever it is, it seems to be working, and I'm going to leave it at that. And now about that broken ornament. I'll sweep and you scoop."

"Deal."

15

On Thursday, within minutes of two in the afternoon, Kevin Daly parked his remarkably unremarkable, recent model, mid-sized hybrid something-or-other outside the house. Viridienne and Emily and Fitz, who had driven his own car this time and was wearing his preferred jeans and Irish sweater, all stepped out onto the front porch to greet him. He'd called earlier to confirm the arrangements, and now, with a size-able Christmas floral arrangement in his arms, he made his way up the front walk toward the house.

The few inches of snow that had fallen earlier in the week remained only in memory and in a few swept and shoveled heaps along the walk. Even those were fast disappearing. The fickle New England weather had reversed itself, and the outside temperature was almost spring-like. Fitz had once quoted Twain, who advised, "If you don't like the weather in New England now, just wait a few minutes," and he was right. Viridienne wondered if they would have a white Christmas or a warm wet Christmas this year, and she knew there was absolutely no predicting which.

Kevin flicked a glance at Fitz and held out the flowers to Emily and Viridienne. "I won't be here for the holiday itself, but I thought I'd like to give you all a little something in gratitude for your letting me settle in early. If you keep these watered, they should last well into the new year."

"That's really nice of you, Kevin. Thank you. I'll take them in and put them on the dining room table. We don't have anything Christmassy in there, just a couple of red candles I got at the dollar store, so this will be perfect. I'll take good care of them, I promise." Viridienne took the arrangement and turned back into the house.

Fitz held out his hand to Kevin. "Well, then, my friend, here we are again. I knew you were coming today, and I had a few extra minutes, so I thought I'd swing by and give you a hand with your things. I don't know about you, but whenever I move anything from one place to another, the boxes seem to multiply in the back of the car. Not only that, no matter how well I tape them, one always seems to explode."

"Amen, brother," said Kevin. "It's very good of you, but you needn't have bothered. I move around a lot, so anything I want to keep with me fits in the back of my car. You know, just in case I need to make a speedy escape." He paused and added, "Joke."

Fitz would not be put off. "Like I said the other day, many hands make light work. So let's get on with it." He tactfully made no mention of the flicker of irritation that crossed Kevin's face but cheerfully walked past him and out to his car. Daly wasn't kidding. When he stepped through the door, Fitz could see three taped boxes, two suitcases and a multi-wheeled under-the-airplane-seat computer case.

"I've got my hanging clothes in a couple of bags folded in the trunk. This is it. I told you I travel light."

"You weren't kidding," said Fitz.

Kevin laughed. It was genuine this time. He held up a reassuring hand. "Hey, man, I don't want you to think I'm a weirdo drifter or anything. You know, like that Jack Reacher character that Lee Child writes about? Have your read those books? The hero's a drifter with a nose for trouble. He carries nothing with him but the clothes on his back, a wallet and toothbrush. Not me. I have a storage unit up in Maine near where my mother lives. One of these days I will think about settling down, and when I do, I'll have my creature comforts up there waiting for me."

"Childs is a good writer," said Fitz. "Now hand me one of those boxes, and we'll get this over and done with. I suspect we can prevail upon the ladies of the house to make us a cup of tea."

Again, Kevin held up his hand. "I'm afraid this is going to have to be a hit-and-run, but I do appreciate the invite. I'll settle for good later in the week between Christmas and the New Year, when I get back from my mother's. Exact date TBA. The plan for today is to drop all this stuff off and pick up a couple of keys."

"A couple? How many do you need?" The words were out of Fitz's mouth before he knew it. A professional reflex.

"I thought I'd ask Viridienne for a rear door key, as well. I'll be parking in the back, and I can just slip in and out without bothering anyone or disturbing their privacy."

"Makes sense to me." Fitz didn't know whether this was a good idea or a bad one, but at that very moment, he wasn't in a position to do or say anything about it. It sounded perfectly reasonable, and in similar circumstances, he would very likely have done the same.

He might be a poet and a dreamer in his off-duty hours, but on duty or off, Patrick Fitzpatrick was always on guard, watching and listening. It was one of the things that made him so good at what he did.

Once Kevin's things were in and stacked with almost military precision, he thanked Fitz for the help, took possession of his keys, front and back, wished them all a happy holiday and took his leave.

Emily waved him off and tactfully headed upstairs, telling Fitz and her sister that she was going to hang out on her computer so Viridienne and Fitz could have the kitchen table to themselves. Neither of them tried to stop her and did as they were bidden. Fitz slipped his arm through hers, and the two of them headed towards the kitchen.

16

"So, Detective Fitzpatrick, now that you've had a second close encounter with our soon-to-be-lodger, what do you think?" Viridienne quickly had a cup of lethally strong tea sitting in front him. He sat and grabbed onto it with both hands, took a long swallow and blew out a sigh of contentment before saying, "I'd say he's passed all the tests. He's clean, very orderly, likes to read. He's not too garrulous, but he's not without words when called upon to use them. I'll give him a pass." He looked down into his tea for a moment. "I have to be honest and say that there is something poking at the back of my brain, but I don't think it has anything to do with him. I think it's just me being a man watching another man move into your house." He held up his hand. "I know, I have no right to feel that way. I don't own you." He dropped his voice. "But you may have noticed that I enjoy your company, and I'm seeking more and more of it these days."

She smiled and reached for his hand. "He's a lodger, Fitz. Think of him as an electric bill or a heating bill. We are in the business of renting rooms to people, and not to put too fine a point on it, we can use the money. You are the only man in my life, and I don't see that changing."

"I'm getting all unnecessary again, Vid. It's just me being protective, or maybe it's possessive or more likely a little bit of both. It's a guy thing. He'll be okay, and so will I."

"Fitz?" Viridienne looked him directly and said softly, "Speaking of the guy thing, I'll remind you of what I said to you before. Should you ever be so inclined, I wouldn't say no if you wanted to stay the night…once in a while… now and then…maybe even tonight."

The man sitting across from her did a double-take and almost dropped his tea. She watched his face go from pink to crimson.

"Shall I take that as a yes, then?" she teased.

He nodded and after a long pause said, "Jaysus, Mary and Joseph, yes, and what am I going to tell my mam?"

Viridienne rolled her eyes. "Your mam, wasn't born yesterday, and when she was, it wasn't under a cloud of unknowing. You weren't adopted, were you?"

Still bright pink, he shook his head. "Um, may I ask what brought this on? Not that I'm disagreeing with the idea, mind you, but why now? Something to do with the Christmas spirit?"

"Not likely, Fitz, I'm an atheist, remember? No, I decided I'm ready to take this to another level, and knowing that you are so respectful of my personal history, I realized you might never take the next step. So I just did."

"Dear God, woman, it's not like I haven't thought about it … thought about it a lot, in fact." He looked away. "I will spare you the details. No, it's more like I'm Irish and

Catholic on top of that. You know, mortal sin and all that nonsense."

"So, have you just changed your mind, and you're telling me no?"

Fitz clapped both hands to his head. "God-in-heaven, no, Vid. More like I'm lost for words, gob-smacked, bowled over, happier than a clam at high tide..." He stopped mid-sentence and asked.

"What about Emily?"

"She wasn't born yesterday either, and the doors in this house are like lead, totally soundproof. I know, because I've had a summer full of renters. None of them told me they were monks or nuns, and I never heard a thing. Sex happens. Emily and I are not joined at the hip. One day she'll no doubt find someone special herself, and then she can lock her door."

Fitz, growing redder by the second, didn't look convinced, but neither did he look like he was going to turn down the offer.

"So, my friend, would you like to stay?"

"I, uh, don't have my toothbrush." He winked at her.

"We keep extras for the guests, soap and deodorant, too."

He threw up his arms. "All right, then, but only if you insist."

"I insist. Now then, what shall we all have for supper? It's getting to be that time."

"I get supper as well? Should I make a run to the package store and get a bottle of wine? And what are you going to tell your sister?"

"Wine would be lovely. Any color, I still don't know much about what goes with what, when it comes to wine, and I don't drink enough to care one way or the other."

17

So, teddy bear-boy, are you ready for a second round of holiday cheer with even more benefits? What are you doing on Christmas Eve? Better, what are WE doing on Christmas Eve? (Is there any question?) Do you think we can find someplace away from the shepherds and the angels and make some heavenly music of our own????? Tell me yes and tell me where to meet you and I'll be there with bells on. Christmas is so full of surprises. Let's take off the wrappings and make it happen.

18

Call it modesty or cowardice, or perhaps it was more like don't ask, don't tell, but early the next day Detective Fitz was up, dressed, shaved, brushed, flossed and gone before the sky was fully light—long before anyone else in the house, including the cat, was awake and out of bed. It was December twenty-first, the day of the Winter Solstice, so at seven in the morning the sky was just growing light. As a courtesy he left the coffee pot filled and ready to go for Viridienne and her sister. Then, with an oversized travel mug full of tea clamped in one hand and his car keys in the other, he walked softly toward the front entrance of the house.

So as not to wake the sleepers, he took great care not to let the heavy oak door slam behind him. It was only when he was standing outside on the porch that he realized that while the new lodger might have two keys to that house, he, the man who had just vacated the landlady's bed, didn't even have one. He was faced with a new ethical question. Should he ask for one straight away or

wait until, or even if, one was offered? Fitz was not a little
irritated in thinking that the renter, a stranger really,
should have not one but two keys, and himself, an officer
of the law, no less, was keyless. He snorted and thought,
get hold of yourself, my boy. You don't own her, and you
also have, among other duties of the day, a crime to inves-
tigate and a vicious murderer to find. It's time to stop
your belly-achin' and get on with it. You are a lucky,
lucky man.

With the lecture-to-self over and done with, Fitz all but
skipped down the front walk to his car. He was grinning like
a Cheshire cat from ear to ear, a very happy Cheshire cat.
The outside temperature had plummeted overnight, and
the snow melt puddles were now sheets of glass that shone
up from the pavement. He needn't be worried about slipping, though. The man was walking on air.

Inside the house Viridienne, wrapped in her own smiles
as well as a grey plaid bathrobe that complimented her hair,
hit the start button on the coffee maker. She, too, had a full
day ahead of her. With a week to go until Christmas, she
was still filling orders. She would be spending the first part
of the day in her studio and the afternoon in the car, delivering the goods.

She was a successful practicing artist now, and to both
her surprise and mild dismay, it was a mixed blessing. She
had a ready market for what she produced, the dream of
almost any artist, but with it came the pressure of
producing the work these people wanted. There was little
time for self-expression in the weeks leading up to the holidays and then to when the summertime artisan fairs began.
Still, thinking about the man who'd left the coffee pot filled
and ready to go, she smiled her own Cheshire smile. Viridienne was happier than she'd ever imagined possible, and if

this was what all the songs and poems were about, she'd take it.

Her dreamy lassitude was interrupted by the simultaneous arrival of her sister and the cat. The cat, because he was a cat, made no mention of the fact that her bedroom door had been closed all night, and he couldn't get in despite his best efforts at rattling the doorknob and piteous wailing, sometimes both at the same time.

Emily said nothing, because it was clear from her lack of direct eye contact with her sister that she didn't know what to say. She covered her awkwardness by making a great show of looking for her favorite coffee mug and talking to the cat. Viridienne was taking amused advantage of the situation by saying nothing and letting the lengthening silence shimmer in the air between them. Finally, she looked up at her sister, nodded and giggled.

"It's okay, Em, you can look at me. Fitz did stay the night, and yes, the earth did move, and it's likely he and it will do so again from time to time, but he's not moving in. I promise you that."

Emily turned to her sister, coffee mug in hand. "Why would you say that, Vid? He's your friend, and it's your house. You're my sister, and I want you to be happy. If he makes you happy, then go for it." She paused, still looking directly at her sister. "He's a good man, and he's his own person, Vid. I like him. I repeat, go for it. You deserve it."

"Baby steps," said Viridienne, "little bitty ones, and just one at a time."

AT PLYMOUTH POLICE HEADQUARTERS, Fitz and his investigative partner, Alison Grey, were seated across from each other in their shared office. They were still struggling to make sense of the murder they were investigating and still making very little progress. The deliberate taking of a human life was both horrific and disturbing, and they were both doing their best to get beyond their personal feelings. They had work to do, and to do it well, they had to remain professionally detached. Getting personally involved was a deterrent to clear thinking.

The task at hand was to collect and analyze the facts of the crime and see if they could piece together some sort of a picture or a pattern that would one day lead them to the killer. Clearly this was a hate crime. The victim, a well-known Plymouth native and outspoken member of the LBGTQ community, had been viciously murdered and his body dumped off South Point, a rocky glacial leftover that jutted out into the ocean south of Plymouth harbor. The victim's family, the man's husband, and members of the town council were devastated and wanted answers. The pressure was mounting.

The mystery was two-fold. It was clear from the *post mortem* that the victim had recently had sex, and the murder took place either during or immediately after the encounter. Was it a lover's quarrel gone too far? Or was it what they both suspected, a one-off, targeted killing by someone who hated this man? Or was it another in what might be methodical targeted serial killings of gay men. This was an unfolding mystery primarily confined to a network of investigative teams tracking sex and hate crimes across the country and connected to one another through the internet.

The only pattern that had emerged thus far was that the victims were all men of means, well known and respected in their communities. The victims under investigation were not nameless, homeless men or even male prostitutes. They were not, in the judgmental eyes of many people, throw-aways. These were professional, educated, respected men who, for whatever reason, decided to stray from the familiar and go out on a date with a stranger, a date from which they would never return.

Computer records showed all of the men were active on social media, and most had accounts, sometimes more than one, on gay social and dating sites which would suggest how the killer might have made initial contact with his victims. However, extensive forensic investigation of the victims' computers and their cell phones turned up nothing that would lead investigators to the person that killed them.

Alison leaned forward on her elbows and rested her chin in her hands.

"Looks like we're getting nowhere fast, my friend. We have a definite pattern in the killings themselves and even the spacing of the clusters and the kind of men that are being targeted, but that's it. We get this far and no further."

"What's bothering me the most is that if this is one of those serial murders, and it certainly has all of the earmarks, and if the murderer follows his established pattern, he's going to go after somebody else within days. We don't have much time."

Grim-faced, Alison nodded. "The one thing I see that isn't made much of in any of the other reports, is that all of the victims had families. Some were married to women, some married to or in a committed relationship with another man, and it would appear that they were secretly looking for a little something on the side, something that they didn't want anyone at home to know about."

"And it killed them."

She nodded. "People stray, it's human. It's a fact that men stray more than women and take greater risks when they do. Maybe it's the excitement of taking a risk. Who knows? My father used to say, 'A different horse in the stable.'"

Fitz nodded. "So, what do we do? We can't stake out every bar and alley in Plymouth. Although many of them have surveillance cameras now, and that's something, it's likely to be too little too late if it's after the fact."

Alison, her lips in a flat line, said, "We're going around in circles, Fitz. I think we need a coffee break."

The two stood. Fitz groaned and stretched while Alison reached for her purse.

"You choose. The coffee machine downstairs or shall we go for something beyond the pale?" he asked.

"Beyond the pale?" She gave him a quizzical look.

"Pale, the outer castle wall?"

"Of course," she said. "I knew that."

In what appeared to be an abrupt change of mood, Fitz straightened up, opened the office door with a flourish, bowed to his partner and began humming "Jingle Bells."

Alison gave him a curious look. "Counting the days, are you?"

"I am," said Detective Fitzpatrick.

"Big family time, is it?"

"You might say that."

19

In what seemed like no time at all, the days were accomplished, and Christmas Eve, with its drums and whistles, strings of fairy lights, canned music and real live silver bells, was delivered most fully unto them. Viridienne, her sister Emily and Fitz, by what he would call the grace of God and Vivienne would refer to as damned good luck, were spending it together. Fitz would take his mother to the five o'clock Mass and then head over to La Vie en Rose. The plan was to have Christmas presents around the fire, then dinner, and after that they would all walk down the hill to St. Peters for the midnight Mass.

When Fitz first mentioned this as a possibility and then actually went ahead and invited her, Viridienne's knee-jerk response was a quick, "Thanks but no way in hell." Then she reconsidered. In the spirit of getting to know this man, a man she really liked, maybe even loved, she decided it would do no harm if she attended a church service with him. Once. His Catholic faith was a huge part of his life, his history and his family culture. Viridienne wanted no part of it for herself, but she did want at least to understand and have some respect for it as a courtesy to him.

Until then, the only church service she had ever been to in her life was her friend Rose's Greek Orthodox funeral. Not a happy first experience or memory. She pushed it away. That was then, and this is now, and it would be her first real true Christmas in her great big beautiful house with people she loved. Besides, from everything she'd heard, Jesus was an okay guy; he just wasn't God. So everybody gets to celebrate his birthday and have a good time doing it, whatever they think of him. She could live with that. Okay then, Bring it on, all of it.

On the afternoon before Christmas Eve, with her cooking done, Viridienne was the very picture of domesticity. She was sitting cross legged in front of a low fire, putting the finishing touches on her tree-top creation. DT was splayed out on his back, four legs akimbo, basking in the delicious warmth. Looking down at him, she couldn't help but think that bringing all this happiness back into the house might be a new beginning for all of them. The darkness was behind her. The tragic memories of Rose and how she died were real enough, but they had been resolved and were now packed away in a safe place. From now on this house and the people who lived in it along with the present and future guests who would cross the threshold would be part of a whole new chapter.

The pleasant image was interrupted by her phone, caller unknown. She considered not answering it, but curiosity got the better of her.

"Viridienne."

She recognized the voice of Kevin Daly.

"I just thought I'd call and wish you a Merry Christmas."

"Why, thank you Kevin. The same to you and to your mother, as well.

"That's kind of you. She doesn't get out much now, so every little thing pleases her. I'll be sure to tell her."

"As long as I have you, do you know what day next week you'll be moving in?"

"Actually, I've decided to stay up here with my mother until after the New Year. I think I need to spend a little more one-on-one time with her so I can really see how she's doing. She always says she's fine, but I want to know for myself. Anyway, that's all for now. I don't want to interrupt your evening. I'll call or text you next week when I know my ETA."

"ETA?"

"Estimated time of arrival. Travel slang. I travel a lot. Anyway, Merry Christmas to you and your sister."

Viridienne couldn't really explain why she felt a mild sense of relief in hearing this, but neither did she give it much thought. She and Emily were delighted to greet and welcome every single guest who arrived at their door, and when each one paid their bill and departed, they both breathed a little sigh of relief as they waved them off and turned back into their private space. They did like having the place to themselves, but they had bills to pay and food to buy and a car, disreputable as it was, to maintain, but maybe one day? It was all a matter of balance and perspective, wasn't it? Everything in moderation, right? Time would tell whether Kevin Daly would be a one-time experiment in extended rentals, something they might even advertise for in the future during the low occupancy months, or a one-time, one-off not to be repeated.

The phone on the sofa beside her buzzed for a second time, signaling a text. It was from Fitz saying that he wouldn't be there until after seven that evening. His mother asked him to stay on for a cup of tea after the five o'clock Mass. He signed it,

"See you later, Detective S. Claus."

She chuckled and tapped a response.

"No problem, Detective S. Claus. Just remember to park the reindeer on the side roof. You know what the neighbors are like! …V."

ONE OF THE unexpected side-benefits of her growing relationship with this winsome Irishman was humor and having fun simply for its own sake. Too many years of fighting for survival and reclaiming her own personhood after leaving the cult had left her with little time for play.

It wasn't much past seven-thirty that evening when S. Claus, AKA Fitz, arrived at the door, and the merriment began. First on the schedule were glasses of wine and presents around the fire. Fitz began the giving ritual by handing each woman an envelope in which was a Christmas card containing a yearlong on-street parking permit for the town of Plymouth.

"I know it's not romantic or sentimental or even festive, but it is useful, and it has the added benefit of my not having to fix any parking tickets you two might incur."

"These must have cost you an arm and a leg," gasped Emily, who was clearly delighted.

Fitz winked, touched the side of his nose with his index finger and said, "Don't ask."

DT, taking no notice of the humans in the room, was busily entertaining himself attacking the tissue paper and the sticky-bows and climbing in and out of empty gift bags.

Emily, clever and generous as all get-out, but not at all

the crafty type, gave Fitz a gift card to a local book store tied to a pocket-sized nip bottle of Jameson's labelled, 'For use in case of emergency." She gave Viridienne a gift certificate to a well-known fiber and yarn shop and cleverly placed the small envelope containing it inside an oversized and beautifully woven Romanian Gypsy basket for her ever-present knitting. In seconds, DT spotted the basket with his one good eye, claimed ownership on the spot and spent the rest of the evening crawling in, out and over it.

Viridienne, beyond happy, was contentedly waiting for her own time to come. As usual she'd made her gifts, and when it was her turn, she pulled them out from under the tree and handed two poorly wrapped, oddly shaped packages to Emily and two more, smaller in size, to Fitz.

Emily, excited as a child, tore the larger one open to find a knitted lace shawl made in her favorite colors, a variety of blues and greens. She immediately wrapped it around her shoulders and then attacked the smaller parcel, a piece of blue sea glass, wound in gold wire and strung on a thin gold chain.

"It was all I could afford," said Viridienne. She was thoroughly enjoying her sister's unbridled enthusiasm. "I'll get you the matching earrings for your birthday. I got it at the gallery. I know the woman who makes them. We did a swap!"

Then she turned to Fitz to watch him open his packages. She was full of excitement and happy anticipation as he methodically opened first one, and then the other. Each contained a single knitted sock. The two made a perfectly matched soft grey-green tweed pair that would come well up on his legs. Fitz peeled off his shoes and socks and put them on at once. Appropriately enough, they fit as though they'd been made for him. He looked down at them, twisting his feet this way and that, admiring them from all angles and smiling broadly.

"Just the thing for days like this. It's freezing out there tonight. I can't tell you how cold my feet get in the winter."

"Actually, you did tell me. That's why I made them." She winked.

There was another package on the floor next to where Fitz was sitting, but he made no move toward it. Viridienne waited, and when she couldn't stand it any longer, she pointed to it and said, "Uh, what's that? Have we left something out?"

He grinned and once again touched the side of his nose with his forefinger. "Not a bit of it, Miss Nosey. This is for the two of you, and I will present it when we get back from Mass."

"Will you at least give us a hint?" asked Emily.

"That I will not," said the detective, looking down at his watch, "and I hope I'm not pushing my luck when I say this, but if we are going to get to the church on time, hadn't we better put something in our stomachs pretty soon? If we don't, we won't be able to hear the music for the groaning and the grumbling."

"Go and seat yourselves in the dining room," said Viridienne "It's all ready to go. All I have to do is bring it out. We'll have the main meal now and our dessert when we get back. I made a real Bouche de Noel, that's a Yule-log cake. I saw the recipe online. It looked like fun, and it was, but it turned out to be hard work. It came out great, though, and I have to say I'm proud of it."

"Would you like me to get these flowers out of the way and put them over there on the sideboard? That way we can see each other while we eat."

"Good thinking, detective, even if you are off duty."

"Off duty is an oxymoron in my business. I may not be on the clock 24/7, but if something happens and I'm called in, I go, no questions asked. Let's just hope it doesn't."

"Fingers crossed," said Emily, holding up her two hands with all fingers crossed and double crossed.

"Quiet, girl. Don't tempt fate. Let's have our dinner and not think about anything procedural other than getting to the church in time to get a good seat."

"Amen to that," said Viridienne.

20

In one of the larger and louder bars on the main street in the center of town, a man sitting by himself at a table for two kept glancing toward the door. The red and green twinkling lights strung over the bar give his face, what could be seen of it in the shadows, a distinctly ghoulish appearance in the half-filled room. Christmas Eve in a bar is one of the loneliest places on earth with the possible exception of a nursing home. It is, however, a place to go when you have nowhere to go, and you need to go somewhere so you won't be completely alone. A place where you can go, people-watch, maybe get lucky and find a kindred soul to talk to for a while, and have a few drinks to dull the pain. Then you can stagger home or up the street and sit with the other lonely drunks in the last row of St. Peter's for midnight Mass.

21

F itz and his two ladies were bundled up and ready to step out the door when Fitz held up his hand and stopped them.

"I was going to suggest we walk." Fitz pointed to his feet. "Me with my new socks and all, but it's colder than the hammers of hell out there. Even though the church is only down the hill and around the corner, I think we should drive. You can't even breathe in this kind of cold."

Viridienne and Emily did not need convincing. It was already late for them. Ordinarily at this hour, they would already be in bed or preparing to be. It was the Christmas excitement that kept them going—that and the secret surprise as yet to be opened and the divinely beautiful and sweet dessert that awaited them when they got back. Viridienne held open the door, and Fitz pulled out his keys and tossed them in the air. They jingled like silver bells … in the city.

He was right, it was bitterly cold. The night air hit the three of them like a cruel slap across the face. Inside the car wasn't much better, but at least there was no wind to add insult to injury. The drive to the church took all of five minutes, and they were early enough so there was still plenty of room in the parking lot.

Once inside the softly lighted church interior, Fitz genuflected and crossed himself before entering a pew. Viridienne and Emily slipped in beside him. Viridienne, with her artist's eye, was taking it all in. It was richly beautiful but nowhere near as lavishly ornate as the Greek Orthodox Church she remembered from Rose's funeral. This was a well-proportioned space with good acoustics, filled with statues and pictures of men and women, all who appeared to be suffering. She would try to remember to ask Fitz about this when they got back.

But now, the entrance of a beautifully costumed priest, followed by several white-robed attendants, all carefully stepping around the mountains of poinsettias piled up around the altar, made it clear that something important was about to begin.

22

The man sitting at a table by himself looked up. After a moment's hesitation he signaled another man standing just inside the door to join him. The newcomer stopped at the bar, ordered two drinks and carried them to the table.

"Merry Christmas."

"I was hoping you'd come."

The new arrival set down the two drinks and dropped into the other chair. "Why ever wouldn't I? No one should be alone at Christmas, don't you agree?"

23

Inside the crowded sanctuary of St. Peter's, the air smelled of incense, bodies pressed too closely together and not a little boozy breath. Viridienne was seated on a hard wooden pew next to Fitz, holding his hand and watching as an interested observer the age-old ritual unfold. The music was lovely, much of it familiar; the incense did not make her sneeze; and the ritual movements, the bowing and the turning, the coming and going of the men and women on the altar, was as carefully rehearsed and harmonious as any well-choreographed ballet. She was watching it as she would any professionally staged performance, and she was enjoying it as such. She was not in any way overcome by the Holy Spirit or seized with a desire to run up the center aisle and throw herself at the feet of Jesus. She was a detached and courteous observer, watching it all unfold from a safe distance.

The church itself was full to bursting, and she recognized quite a few familiar faces from around town and the Art gallery. She was almost to the point of deciding that she could do this once a year for Fitz when she felt the buzz of his cell phone against her thigh. He let go of her hand, pulled the phone out of his pocket and read the message.

"Oh Christ!" he mumbled. "I have to go. There's been an incident on Burial Hill, the old cemetery behind Town Square. Can you and Em get back home by yourselves?"

Viridienne waved away his concern. "Of course. It's ten minutes away. We can walk or more likely hitch a ride with someone. You go." To Emily's questioning look, she whispered only, "Police call."

Fitz got to his feet, edged his way past the two seated women, hastily genuflected and wasted no time getting out the rear door and back to his car.

At the end of the service, with the last strains of "Silent Night" still lingering in the rafters above them, Viridienne and Emily caught a ride home with a friend from the gallery.

Once home, Viridienne briefly considered turning on the fire in the sitting room but just as quickly decided against it. She was beyond tired. The police call had taken away too much of the holiday energy and magic, and it seemed far too late to try and rekindle it.

"What do you think it was that called him away?" asked Emily. She was curled into her favorite spot on the sofa.

"He probably won't tell me. He's not supposed to talk about work, but if it is really big, it'll be on the news. Do you want to turn on the TV and take a look?"

Emily shook her head. "Not really. The TV will be full of fillers, repeats and Christmas stuff. It's been a really nice night, so why spoil it? Like you said, if it is bad, we'll find out soon enough, and if it isn't, maybe Fitz will tell us." She yawned broadly. "I vote for bed, and I vote for it now. We can catch up on the news tomorrow."

"Agreed." Viridienne scanned the room. "Where's DT?" He always comes to the door when I come home. I swear that cat thinks he's a dog."

At the sound of his name the cat, with his good eye wide open, slowly came out from behind the sofa with a Christmas sticky bow in his mouth.

"He must have been guarding his latest treasure. Come on, you, it's bedtime for cats. You going up, Em?"

She nodded, and then added. "In a couple of minutes, Vid. I just want to check my email."

24

In the ICU at South Coast General Hospital, a badly beaten man was lying motionless in a medically induced coma as the emergency staff clustered around him, fighting to save his life. It was clear that he'd been sexually attacked, and whoever did it had tried to strangle him. But the victim, Winslow Bishop, was a man whose face was familiar to many of them as a long-time member of Town Council and a regular Sunday presence at the local Methodist church.

The attack had been vicious, but somehow he'd managed to break loose and scream for help. The commotion attracted the attention of a trio of passersby who called 911 and attempted to intervene and, in so doing, scared off the attacker. Rather than trying to give chase, the good Samaritans covered him with one of their coats, performed CPR and stayed with the victim until the police and the ambulance arrived.

Because it was far too cold outside to conduct any kind of serious interview at the crime scene, Fitz brought the witnesses back to the station to thaw out and answer some questions.

After they were all seated, he thanked Alison for coming in on Christmas Eve. Then he thanked the three men for their quick thinking and their willingness to stay with the injured man after they made the 911 call. He first took their names and contact information and then asked the obvious question. "Why, on Christmas Eve, were you three walking around in one of the oldest burial grounds in America, the final resting place of some of the very first of this country's undocumented immigrants?"

Joey, clearly the leader of the three, was the first to speak. "Well, we'd been to a house party, and we'd all had a couple—uh, make that more than a couple—so we decided to walk home by way of the hill. You know, sober up a little in the cold air and take look at the harbor and the lights on the way. It was that or go to church." He shook his head. "We decided to head up the hill, and it's a good thing for that poor bastard that we did. Right time, right place for us, wrong place, wrong time for him. The poor guy was half naked. He woulda froze to death in the cold." He grimaced. "None of my business what people do behind closed doors, but this was sick."

"Can you tell us anything at all about the attacker?"

Joey shook his head. "Not much. It was dark, and there were trees and gravestones in the way. I can't even say that I saw what he was wearing. He brightened. "Okay, one thing maybe, he didn't limp. Not much is it? I mean, he ran away really fast."

"It's better than nothing," said Alison, but she didn't go on to say why.

When they finished, Alison offered to take the men home. Fitz, well beyond sleep, went off to the hospital. He went, not in hopes of speaking to the poor man, but simply to see what he looked like, or used to look like, and maybe say a little prayer, as well.

On the way to the hospital, Fitz thought about Burial Hill and why the attacker chose it for the scene of the crime. Or maybe he didn't. A local would know it was dark and out of the way but accessible on foot. That it was likely to be on anyone's watch list. No CCTV cameras. It's not even that well lit. It's a popular tourist attraction but not on Christmas Eve with the temperature in the single numbers. He knew that it dated back to the 17th century. More recently, besides being on all the tourist maps, it had become an off-street gathering place for the local homeless population. It was listed as the second oldest burying ground in America and the final resting place of several of the founding settlers of Plymouth Colony, the storm-tossed Pilgrims and seekers of religious freedom.

Fitz, who besides being a cop and a closeted poet, was an amateur historian, made a note to self to look up the name and location of the first burial ground.

25

W hen the attacker realized he'd misgauged the strength of his victim, he took off running over the crest of the cemetery, down the street on the other side and dived into his car. Once inside, rather than make any noise by starting the engine, he threw it into neutral and coasted down the hill before actually turning the key all the way. He knew he could do nothing that might attract attention. The police were out now, looking for a nameless attacker as well as patrolling the streets for drunk drivers, all too commonplace on Christmas Eve.

He was shaking so badly he could barely drive, but he needed to keep moving. A man, sitting alone in a car, parked by the side of the road on Christmas Eve, was an open invitation to police inquiry. He might as well put a sign on the car. "Here I am, come get me."

He'd failed. It was the first time since he had begun this grizzly campaign, and he was completely unnerved. It was always the same, three hits and move on, an unholy trinity for a man who hated God and everything to do with him.

The God he was trying to please and never could, because of the living filth he was made of. Not clay, but filth, excrement, a vile excrescence. One day he would end it all, but not before he got rid of as many of his own kind as he could. But now, he reasoned, picking up speed, the only way forward was forward. His only recourse was to finish what he'd started.

He failed because he hadn't anticipated the strength and agility of his latest victim. Everything else, the anonymity, the absence of any manner of electronic paper trail, the ease of the hook-up, it all worked until it didn't. He willed his heart to stop hammering against his ribs and forced himself to count out his breathing and pay attention to the road. He knew his protective gloves and his dark trousers were wet with blood, the victim's DNA, and if discovered, they would be his arrest warrant and death sentence. The clothing and the gloves were disposable. The question was where?

The man drove on, breathing more easily now. He knew where to go and what to do.

26

Fitz picked up one of the visitor's chairs and set it down next to the bed. With both shock and dismay, he recognized the man lying on the bed: Winslow Bishop. He was not, as he had earlier surmised, a known member of the local GLBTQ community. He was a prominent and respected business man, a member of the local Rotary Club, married with children, and had a secret life that on Christmas Eve had damn near killed him.

The man in the bed was unconscious, breathing regularly courtesy of a machine, but at least he was breathing. His color around the darkening bruises was not great, but it wasn't grey either. Over the years of doing this kind of thing, discovering bodies and dealing with almost but not quite dead people, he'd learned to recognize the signs and read the indicators. The machines recording and announcing everything about the man and his bodily functions indicated that his heart rate was weak but regular, his oxygen level was good, and his blood pressure was low but stable. The machine could not tell him whether there had been a brain injury from the massive blow to the back of the head. So many questions to ask on a Christmas Eve when most people wanted more than anything to be home and warm and safe and surrounded by family.

He learned at the desk that the man's wife was, right now, on her way to the hospital and by default, and as necessary to the investigation, he would be the one to ask the probing and invasive questions of a shocked, outraged and frightened woman. Chances were, if history and prior experience was any kind of a teacher, she'd have few answers. At first. Later she would have questions, lots of them. But would she ever dare to ask them? He crossed himself and whispered a quick prayer for the man in the bed in front of him and for the family that was about to be devastated by what had happened. That was, by the sound of it, approaching the room right this very minute.

The night outside the hospital window kept getting longer and darker. Fitz knew everybody else in town had long since gone to bed and that he would watch the sun rise without ever closing his eyes. His thoughts turned to Viridienne. He wondered briefly what she thought of the midnight Mass and when might he get the chance to ask her. He thought about the still unopened package on the floor of her sitting room next to the sofa. He thought about the uneaten Bouche de Noel and hoped they would save him some. He looked again at the man in the bed and thought of "all the lonely people" and wondered where *did* they all come from? More importantly, where do they all go when the sun comes up in the morning?

27

The man with the bruised and bitten hand and the blood on his trousers was all cleaned up and back in his car. There was one last housekeeping detail to attend to before he could go to bed. He was badly shaken. Failure had not been in his vocabulary. Now it was. With the stained clothing and the bloody gloves, all of it wrapped in several layers of newspaper and tied with a string on the seat beside him, he drove to a vacant parking lot behind one of the largest restaurants in town. There, after doing a double check to make sure he was alone and unobserved, he stuffed the package down into the nearest dumpster as far as he could reach. He chose the closest one on the theory that wait staff and busboys, being inherently lazy, would always use the one nearest the door. He'd worked in restaurants in his early years, and he'd done the very same thing himself. The nearest container would, by default, always be the fullest and therefore the first to be taken away. He was not disappointed. The greasy thing was full and brimming over with fresh garbage.

He rammed the accursed package down past the stinking lobster shells, the soggy French fries and through the globs of tartar sauce and ketchup, past the shiny, limp leaves of unfinished salad and chunks of half-eaten dinner rolls. It was revolting, but it was the perfect disposal. Just more garbage. The trash truck would take it all away the next morning, dump it God knows where, and he could get on with his work.

He was already grooming the man that would have been the third in this series, had he succeeded with this one, but now, because of the aborted mission, he might have to find himself a new mark just to keep the records even. On the other hand, that could be pushing his luck a little too far. He knew he needed to go back and sleep on it before he made any hasty decisions. By now there wasn't much of the night left, and driving alone on the streets of Plymouth on Christmas morning when everyone else in their right minds was safe at home, dreaming of sugar plums and teddy bears and something else, was not wise. He needed to get out of sight, stay out of sight, and find out whatever he needed to know on television.

Watching from the shadows in back of the trash bins, one of Plymouth's drug-ravaged derelicts remained motionless and well-hidden until the stranger got back in his car and drove out of sight. When you lived rough, and you got thrown out of the shelter because you were stoned, but you needed something to eat, word among the brotherhood was that this was one of the best trash bins in town. The restaurant workers filled it up every night, and the trash collectors came and emptied it every morning. The food was fresh, never more than twenty-four hours old, and in this cold-as-hell weather, certainly not rotten.

Just to be on the safe side, the ragged man waited

another ten minutes before slouching toward the container to see what he could find to eat. While he was at it, he would retrieve the package that the stranger in the car had so recently pushed in there. When it got light enough outside to see, he would undo the wrappings and take a look inside. With luck, it might be something he could sell or, at the very least, burn for heat.

28

Detective Fitzpatrick got to his feet and stepped away from the bed when the victim's wife Ginger was escorted into the room. The attendant nurse, a bright young woman with the name Cindy Cantrell on her photo identity badge, guided the white-faced woman to the now vacant chair. Ginger dropped into it and sat wordlessly staring at the motionless stitched and bandaged man lying in the bed. Her husband, beaten almost to death by a man who had lured him to an isolated graveyard on Christmas Eve for sex and then death.

Nurse Cantrell broke into the awkward silence. "Detective, this is Mrs. Ginger Bishop, Winslow Bishop's wife."

Fitz looked at the woman who was clutching the arms of the chair in an obvious attempt at controlling her emotions. Did she know her husband had another life? Some wives do and never speak of it. Or had she been doubly blindsided to learn that her husband had been brutally attacked by a secret lover who was a man. And, was it a lovers' quarrel gone wrong? Or was it planned and deliberately and savagely executed? Was it an attempted murder? These were the questions he needed answers for, and Detective Fitzpatrick loathed what he knew he had to do: start looking for those answers.

"Good evening, Mrs. Bishop." He held out his hand. "I'm so very sorry to make your acquaintance under these terrible circumstances, but I am an officer of the law, and I'm here to help. We are going to find out who did this to your husband. But right now, I'm going to step outside into the hallway for a few minutes so you can have a little time alone with him."

The nurse put her hand lightly on the woman's shoulder. "You do know he's in a medically induced coma because of the brain swelling, and he can't speak. But there is a part of him that will sense your presence. Take your time and simply talk to him softly, or hold his hand or whatever feels right to you. I'll be just outside the door with the detective if you need me."

In the hallway outside his door, Cindy and Fitz stood side by side saying nothing. They didn't need to. They had both been this situation any number of times over their years of serving the town of Plymouth. They knew each other, and they knew the drill, and they didn't get in each other's way.

Leaning against the hospital-green wall, Fitz was lost in thought. The timing could not have been worse for the poor wife. She was in shock, which meant her guard was down. She would have less wherewithal to sidestep his questions about the truth, awkward as it might be. That and as many facts about the man's daily life as he could decently gather would make a significant difference in the progression of the case and the eventual apprehension of the attacker.

"Mrs. Bishop would like to talk to you, Detective."

The nurse beckoned him back into the room. The woman sitting in the chair next to the bed seemed smaller, seemed to have shrunk even further into herself. She looked unspeakably sad.

I hate this, thought Fitz as he picked up another chair and set it down facing her. "Mrs. Bishop. I wonder if you might be able to give me a few minutes and tell me about your husband."

She covered her face with her hands and nodded.

And so he began. What he learned was that Winslow Bishop was a good man, a good husband and an attentive father. "Too busy," she told him, but wasn't that typical these days? He was active in town politics, coached a children's sports team, and they both attended the Methodist Church "when time permitted."

And then she crumpled. "When did he have time...I don't understand...what did I miss?"

Fitz had no direct answers for these and more questions that stumbled out, and he knew better than to try to supply them.

"We need to find the man who did this, Mrs. Bishop, and we'll get on that first thing in the morning. Right now, you need to go home and get some rest."

She fixed him with a cold stare.

"I didn't say sleep, Mrs. Bishop. I said rest. You need to be at home in your own space with your children and your pets, if you have them."

This produced a nod and a wan smile. "A dog and two cats."

"Go home and let them comfort you. I will want to talk to you again but not right now. You've been very helpful, and I know it hasn't been easy. Your husband is a very good man. I know him from town doings. He's done well by this community, and I, for one, will do my best for him." Fitz paused. "Do you need a ride home?"

"If you don't mind, Detective, I'd rather take a cab."

"I understand. I'll get them to call you one. Meanwhile, if anything comes to mind, and I mean anything, that you think has any bearing at all on this, do please make a note of it, and when we get together again, you can tell me, and we can talk about it." He paused. "It's after five in the morning. You've had no sleep. You've had a terrible shock, and it's cold as charity out there. Are you sure I can't give you a lift? At least I'm a familiar face and not a stranger come in out of the dark."

"You're right," she said, softly. "I accept, and I thank you."

When Viridienne and Emily finally surfaced on Christmas morning, they had saved their Christmas stockings to look forward to. Stockings, fresh coffee, a purring cat and some holiday peace and quiet.

Earlier in the month, they'd each bought the other gaudy, sparkly, shoddily-made-in-China Christmas stockings at the dollar store which they filled to bursting with sweet, silly and tender surprises. In a moment of reflection, Viridienne realized that next year she might be wanting to get a third stocking, one that would be appropriate for a man ... more specifically, a police detective. One day at a time, Viridienne, don't get ahead of your socks!

But this was today. Their coffee was fresh and hot, and their first Christmas morning together awaited them. But underneath the happy anticipation, the dark question of what it was that had called Fitz away so abruptly and with such urgency, was still very much on their minds.

"Do you mind if I flip on the local news and see if there's anything about what happened last night?" Viridienne gestured to the TV in the corner opposite the tree.

"I was thinking the same thing. It's still bugging me. Do it."

It took a few minutes to get past the holiday time fillers and the rhyming home-made infomercials, but eventually an earnest looking young reporter on a local station gave them what they were looking for.

"Police in Plymouth are investigating the brutal beating of a man who was attacked and left for dead in that town's historic Burial Hill Cemetery located off Town Square."

The young man on the screen adjusted his glasses, leaned forward and continued. "Authorities have little to go on at present. The victim, still in a coma, is in the critical care unit at South Point General Hospital. The three men that intervened and called 911 very likely saved his life. Right now, it's too soon to say, but he is reported to be in stable condition, and we all need to hope for the best. As we understand it, the rescuers were walking home from a house party and heard what sounded like a fight in the graveyard on the hill. When they investigated and then intervened, they had the presence of mind to call 911 for help, but they could only watch as the attacker ran away. 'It was dark,' they told reporters, 'and we'd had a few, so we really didn't get a real look at the guy. The guy was running like hell.'"

Another glasses adjustment. The TV reporter was clearly still new at this and trying not to act as nervous as he was. The regular staff were all home for the holidays.

"All I can report now is that the case is under investigation and ask that if anyone has information regarding this incident, please call Plymouth Police Headquarters. And now on to the weather for this bright, brilliant and bone chillingly cold Christmas day." He pivoted to the right. "Mary Lou Graves, what do you have in store for us?"

"That's enough of that, Vid, my coffee's getting cold." Emily flicked off the TV, collected the two stockings from the mantel and handed one of them to her sister. "It's nothing to do with us. If there is anything to be told, Fitz may or may not be able to do it. He doesn't usually talk about work." She paused and sighed. "It's just sad to think of somebody, a husband, a father, a big brother, anyone really, getting the bejeesus kicked out of him on Christmas Eve."

"Any day really, it's just that Christmas makes it worse somehow."

Emily nodded, took a healthy swallow of her coffee and picked up her lumpy stocking. DT, hearing the now familiar sound of wrapping paper, galloped into the room, and for the time being, at least, they were safe and sound, and it was all good on the home front.

With the contents of the stocking unwrapped and giggled over, the two sisters were anticipating a quiet afternoon with books, leftovers from the night before, including the Yule log confection, and maybe listening to some Christmas music on the radio.

Emily put down her book. "I'm going to run upstairs and check my email. We can have a bite to eat when I come down."

"Why don't you check it in the office off the kitchen? You don't have to go all the way upstairs, and its closer to the fridge for when we want to eat."

Emily shook head. "Uh uh. That's the business computer. My personal computer is upstairs."

"But if you're only checking your email ..."

Emily gave her sister an odd smile. "A rule is a rule, sister mine, and I made this one. I'm the keeper of the books and records in this establishment, and I do not mix business with pleasure. I won't be long. It's my happy place, Vid. Don't worry, I'm not spending too much time on it. I just have to check in with my Facebook friends and wish them, Merry Christmas. I found you on Facebook, remember. It can't be all that bad."

"I was only asking, Em. What you do and who you talk to online is none of my business. It's only a time-waster if you let it be."

Emily was on her way up the stairs when the doorbell rang. Viridienne opened the door to a hollow-eyed, in-need-of-a shave, visibly exhausted detective.

"Can a weary Irishman get himself a cup of tea on Christmas day?"

"Good heavens, Fitz, you look awful." Viridienne stepped back and pulled him inside and out of the cold.

"You don't say."

"Come on then. Go collapse on the sofa, and I'll be right back with your tea—one cup, two bags, three drops of milk and no sugar." He smiled up at her and, with some effort, lifted his thumb.

When she returned the man was spark out, flopped over on his side and snoring softly. Funny, she thought, with a private smile, I hadn't noticed that he snored. She unfolded a quilt she'd made some years back. It was an experimental design that didn't quite work for display purposes but more than made up for the lack of artistic merit, in warmth and comfort. She spread it gently over the sleeping man, and he never even flicked an eyelid in response. The phrase, "dead to the world" came to mind, but she pushed it away. Maybe "out like a light?" That sounded better.

Knowing Fitz needed some uninterrupted sleep, she decided to tiptoe upstairs and muddle around in her studio for a while and leave him to rest. By the look of him, he was in desperate need of it.

30

Dear Emmaline,

First, of all, Merry_Christmas. I can't begin to tell you how much I wanted to be able spend it with you. Maybe someday. But knowing you are my pen pal and that I can write to you and you'll write back means so much to me right now. I know I chose this line of work. Maybe if I knew how lonely it would be and how restricting, I might have chosen differently. But here I am, and there you are, back home in America. I wish I could see you in person, but I can't even Skype from here. They say it's a security risk. Texting only on an unregistered, throwaway phone. If I can ever get to a public library again, maybe we can set something up. That's how I found you, you know. Sometimes they let us out for good behavior—hahaha —and when I can, I go straight over to the library and onto their computers. That's how I found the mix-and-match site, and there you were, looking up at me. I know it's way past the date, but I'd like to send you a Christmas gift. Nothing big, just a little something I picked up at one of the market stalls here. Ooops, gotta go. Marching orders. Love, Terry

31

Five hours later the diverse occupants of the house on the hill slowly re-entered the land of the living and regrouped in the sitting room. Fitz was still bleary, but at least his color had returned to normal. Emily, a bit pink cheeked, confessed to falling asleep in her chair at the computer. Viridienne, the self-appointed den mother for the day, was clear-eyed and ready for the next chapter, whatever it might be, stood bright-eyed before them.

"Who wants what? Tea, wine, a beer, water? I'm taking orders. Supper will be beautifully arranged leftovers, we've got plenty of those, followed by the cake we've been looking forward to for twenty-four hours."

Fitz held up his hand in defense. "Don't blame me. Duty called, and we all know I'm a slave of duty."

Viridienne rolled her eyes. "It's not like you had a choice, and it will be all the better for the waiting. Beer, tea or wine?"

"A cup of tea, if you please, my dear, followed by a beer, my dear, which I will get for myself before the end of this year, my dear. Meanwhile let's all hope and pray I don't get another call."

"Amen to that," said Emily, "but it's not like you had a choice or anything. We learned what happen on the TV this morning. It sounded terrible. I hope you weren't in any kind of danger."

"My job requires being in danger. Not all the time, mind you, but certainly on a regular basis. You learn to keep your eyes and ears open at all times, even when you are supposedly off duty. It's not exactly something you can turn off, now, is it? I know I can't. Last night was disturbing, but I wasn't in direct danger. Remember, we never know who or what's coming after us, especially after an incident. Somebody remembers what you said or did. That some-body doesn't like it and comes after you. This time, the attacker was well away by the time we arrived."

Viridienne returned carrying a tray with glasses of wine for herself and Emily and a steaming oversized mug of fresh tea for the man on the sofa, who now had his atten-tion focused on the twinkling tree in front of the window. Emily followed his gaze.

"Viridienne Greene, what in holy Mother Mary's blessed name is that thing on the top of your tree?"

"What does it look like?"

"If I knew, I wouldn't be askin' you now, would I?"

"It's a Christmas angel pig. I just finished it this after-noon. Do you like it?"

He double blinked. "You're serious. You're asking me if I like it." He paused, clearly looking for the best words to use in what was quickly becoming a delicate situation. "Um, well…er…why don't you tell me how you came up with such an …unusual idea, and then how you went about getting it to, uh, fly up there? I mean I've heard people say, 'that'll happen when pigs fly,' but I've never seen it actually happen."

Viridienne leaned back against the sofa pillows with her glass in hand and said, "I've named her Evangeline. I took up all the scraps I could find on my studio floor, all of the throwaways, and I turned them into Evangeline." She paused, and her eyes grew shiny. "When I was little, I used to hide away pretty bits and pieces of yarn and cloth and string to play with when no one was looking. Even then I was a scavenger and an artist, only I didn't have a name for it, other than it was forbidden. I think I told you that my mother found my treasure trove and burned it in front of me. I think Evangeline might have just helped me heal from that memory. I made her out of throwaways. I was a throwaway back then."

"When you put it that way, I think she's absolutely beautiful. She's the loveliest, most beautiful and original flying angel pig I ever have seen."

"I think she looks just like you," said her sister.

"No cake for you, missy,"

Fortified by the tea, Fitz made a great show of clearing his throat and getting their full attention before reaching down for the box on the floor beside him.

"Now, then. This is for the two of you. I'd hoped we could have opened it last night. When you do open it, you'll see why." He held it out to the two women.

"Did you wrap it? It's beautiful. I almost don't want to open it."

"I had the people at the Irish Shop where I bought it do it for me. I may be a poet cleverly disguised as a detective, but I'm no gift-wrapper. Besides, a gift is meant to be opened. Come on then."

Inside the box, three items wrapped in bubble wrap and

surrounded with shiny tissue paper were nestled tightly together. Viridienne handed one to her sister, another to Fitz and kept the littlest one for herself. Fitz tried to protest, saying he already knew what it was and what was the use of that, but Viridienne insisted they should do it together. At the count of three each of them carefully removed the wrappings and set the three translucent Irish Belleek porcelain figurines, a Mary, a Joseph and a baby Jesus cradled in a manger, on the coffee table. Fitz was beaming.

"I don't care what you believe or don't believe about God or Jesus, Viridienne, but where I come from, you cannot have Christmas without a nativity scene." He pointed to the delicate grouping. "Belleek anything— dinnerware, figurines, angels, teapots—the whole lot of it, is highly prized amongst the Irish and plenty beyond that as well. If you'll accept it, next year and the years after that I'll get you another piece or two until you have a complete set, animals and all."

When she could trust her voice not to quaver, she sniffed and said, "This kind of thing symbolizes family and tradition to me, Fitz. I didn't have that growing up. We had a misguided mess that tried to pass itself off as a family, but it was a total lie. I will treasure this, what it means and the pieces to come."

No one said a word about the long-term commitment Viridienne's response implied, but not a one of them missed it.

"It's absolutely beautiful, Fitz. Thank you, and while we're about surprises, I have a little something for you. Four little somethings—five really, if you count the thing I tied them to."

She reached into her pocket and pulled out a lanyard she'd woven, to which she'd attached three shiny new house-keys, and one crusty rusty old one. "There's one for the front door, another for back door leading to the parking area, and the third was to kitchen door that opens out to the garden. The last one, the old skeleton key, was probably one of the originals that opened the door to the cellar. That's where we keep the furnace, the electrical box, and a cool room originally used for storing root vegetables."

"That's a lot of keys there, woman. Are you sure?"

She smiled. "I'm sure. I started thinking, if I can give a renter, a man who's a virtual stranger, a set of keys for his convenience and privacy, I can certainly give you the full Monty."

"I accept," said Fitz, closing the keys in his fist and then tucking them away in his pocket.

"Ready for something to eat, everybody? Come on then. Many hands make light work." Emily was up and away into the kitchen.

"Hold on a minute, Viridienne," said Fitz, reaching into his pocket. "Since we're talking about hands, I do have a little something else for you." He held out a tiny package.

Inside was a little gold ring that was made up of two hands holding a heart and topped with a crown. Set in the heart was a tiny diamond. "It's called a claddagh ring. The meaning and the symbolism are all about love, loyalty and friendship. The two hands represent friendship, the heart symbolizes love, and the crown on top is for loyalty. I'm giving it to you as an 'I like you a whole lot,' ring, and I hope you will wear it in that spirit."

She held the ring in the palm of her hand and looked at it, then looked up at the man who had just given it to her.

"Let's see if it fits." He took the ring and carefully slipped it onto the ring finger of her right hand with the heart pointing inwards. "You should wear it on your right hand with the heart pointed inward toward yourself. It's a friendship ring, Viridienne, and I think of you as a very, very special friend. When you wear it on your right hand with the heart pointing toward you like this, it means you are in a relationship with someone. Are you willing to wear it that way, Lady Greensleeves?"

"I am, my special Irish poet detective friend. I am."

Holy Mystery…
What secret sacred holy saint do have to thank for you?
What holy mystery
What twist of fate
That picked up these two mortal threads
And braided them together?
And what might all this shining fabric come to be?
I cannot say
Because it isn't finished yet

32

A s much as he would have preferred to stay the night with Viridienne, the following day was a workday for Detective Fitz. He needed a change of clothes, and he wanted to check in with his mother. But beyond all of that, he needed some time alone to clear his head, and he would have that in his office.

When he did get in, the message light on his desk was blinking. Something from downstairs, no doubt. Alison had asked for the week between Christmas and the New Year off as vacation time to be with her family. She'd made an exception and come in after the Burial Hill attack, as it was now being called, but technically, she was off for the week. Of course, he could use her help. She was damn good at what she did.

But with so many unknowns and the forensics reports still pending, there wasn't anything he couldn't handle on his own for the time being. The officers on the street were asking questions and checking on site surveillance equipment, and needless to say, the local media outlets were in overdrive. The week post-Christmas is a media dead-zone. Well, this year, it almost was, literally. What Fitz knew and the media didn't was that the details of the Burial Hill attack bore an unmistakable resemblance to the South Point murder and to those other clusters of three murders of gay men that had happened elsewhere in the country. What this meant was, while the general public was not likely to be in immediate danger, middle-class gay men who might be out under cover of darkness looking for a hasty anonymous encounter on the side most definitely were.

The red message light continued to wink at him, and a disheveled man, holding a pile of crumpled newspaper, appeared in the open doorway to his office.

"You the guy workin' on the thing that happened on Burial Hill?"

Fitz nodded and waved the sad-looking creature into his office and directed him to a chair. The man smelled even worse than he looked: urine, sweat, garlic and the overwhelming stench of a long unwashed body.

"Let's start with you telling me your name and how can I help you, sir? Would you like a cup of coffee or a glass of water?"

The man shook his head. "My street name's Bongo. I used t'play drums in bands around here 'n' there." His voice trailed off, and he held up the newspapers. "I found this in th' trash behind the Shell and Cracker restaurant on Christmas Eve. I was lookin' for somethin' t'eat when this guy drives up, gets out of his car, and starts stuffin' somethin' inta the bin. Now I'm hidin' in the shadows watchin, and I don't move a muscle. The guy kept lookin' around like he didn't want nobody to see him and then keeps on stuffin' it deeper and deeper. Even pulled some garbage over it to bury it. When he's done, he takes off. I wait a couple more minutes, just to make sure he don't come back, then I go dig it out. I didn't look inside 'til it got light. Like I said, I was hungry. I was really lookin' for food. But I got curious."

The man wiped his dripping nose on his sleeve and Fitz automatically held out the box of tissues he kept on his desk.

"So when it starts t'get light, I open it up and found some clothes and a pair of rubber gloves wit' blood on 'em. Then I heard about what happened in the cemetery on the hill. We hang out there sometimes, y'know."

Fitz nodded. He did know all too well. Many of Plymouth's homeless community slept among the head-stones when they were too drunk or high to be allowed in one of the shelters. Not a few of them died there as well.

"So anyway, the more I thought about it, the more I thought I should give 'em to you guys, so I brought 'em in. Maybe it's something, maybe it's nuthin', but somebody got hurt that night, and somebody was tryin' real hard to hide it."

He lifted up the messy pile and held it out to the detective.

Fitz knew this could easily be a false lead, a pile of bloody clothes from a fight or a domestic assault or from some stupid teenager who got himself into a fight and didn't want his parents to know. Whatever it was, it was someone trying to hide the evidence of a stupid indiscretion, and somebody saw him do it. On the other hand, this could be the real deal, and John Stokes and his men and women in forensics would be able to tell him. Stranger things have happened, and if this was the real deal, he'd soon know. DNA doesn't lie.

"If this is any good, do I get the reward?"

Getting close to the man and not wincing or wrinkling his nose was an effort, but whatever he looked like and however he smelled, he was some mother's child, and he was a human being. Fitz pulled on a pair of protective gloves, took the package and set it on his desk. There was no need to open it any further at the moment. He could see the blood-stained trousers and blood-stained white latex gloves, now only partially covered by the stained and greasy paper.

"Nothing's been said about a reward for evidence, but I will check and see."

Bongo grunted. "You said somethin' about coffee? I could use some ... and maybe a doughnut?" The man in the chair looked hopeful.

There was nothing more in the world that Fitz wanted to do than to get these shattered remains of a man out of his office. Instead, he picked up the phone and asked the person who answered if someone could please bring up a couple of large cups of coffee, several breakfast sandwiches, any flavor, and oh yes, a half-dozen mixed doughnuts, as well.

"Thanks, man."

"No problem, my friend. I was ready for a little something myself." He thought, I'm nobody's fool either, my friend. If I take you out for a meal, and one of your street friends sees us together, it could go badly for you in the future. Who knows, another day, another time, I might just need a street voice to tell me things a so-called decent person might not be willing to say.

"Bongo, can you tell me why you waited almost two days to bring this to us?"

The man squinted up at Fitz through filmy, watery eyes.

"Two days? Been two days already?" He snorted and wiped his nose. "Time kinda gets away from me sometimes. You know ..."

I do know, thought Fitz, and it breaks my freaking heart.

33

Viridienne's phone signaled she had a text message. It was Kevin Daly asking if there was anything she might want him pick up on his way back from Maine—specifically, some tax-free wine and spirits in New Hampshire. Also, he was thinking of coming back early after all, but he would by all means let her know if he was. She texted back a thanks-but-no-thanks on the offer of alcohol and thanked him for letting her know that his plans could change.

She put her phone back on the coffee table and picked up her knitting. She couldn't say why the idea of him coming back early unsettled her, but it did. And if it did, maybe this idea of having a long-term renter might be a one-off trial run, a learning experience to be crossed off the list in any future planning.

She realized it wasn't Kevin's fault. He was more than courteous. It was her problem, and she knew it. Maybe it was her past baggage with men in The Society of Obedient Believers. Maybe it was her deepening relationship with

Fitz that was making her a little anxious on all fronts. It's not as if she would be alone in the place with a stranger. Her sister lived there with her, and Fitz would there in minutes if she called him. Whatever it was, she would see this one through and then re-think the idea in conference with her sister and her…well, what was Fitz now? A boyfriend? A significant other? A gentleman caller with benefits? She looked down at the little ring on her hand and smiled to herself. Take it one day at a time, Viridienne. Go easy on yourself. All will be revealed.

AFTER FEEDING Bongo and offering him the use of one of the showers downstairs, Fitz dug around in the clean clothing bins they kept on hand for some of their overnight visitors. When Bongo emerged from the shower, Fitz handed him a stack of clean clothing: heavy jeans, a bright red hooded sweatshirt, fresh underwear, clean white socks and a pair of sturdy shoes, all of which, more or less, fit. He was able to add in a bulky winter jacket which had been hanging in the lost and found room for over a year. Before sending him off, Fitz handed the man a plastic bag containing the remains of the take-out. Then he took two twenty dollar bills out of his wallet, wrapped them around one of his business cards and slipped it all into the man's open hand.

"It's not much, but it's something for your next meal." Fitz knew full well Bongo would use the money to buy drugs and not food.

"You have my contact information. If you remember anything else about what happened that night, or if you hear anything on the streets that you think might help us find the man who did this, please, please contact me, okay?

If you do, I might be able to find a way to get you a real reward." He tapped the man's closed hand. "Right now, this stays just between us, okay?"

Bongo nodded his assent and made straight for the door to the outside. Cold as it was, the warmth of a police station held no promise of the comfort he was seeking.

Fitz watched him go and then wasted no time getting back up to his office so he could take the unpleasant special delivery over to forensics. After that he planned to make a hospital visit and check on how Winslow Bishop was doing and see if he was awake enough to answer a few questions.

Assault, however you look at it, is ugly. In this case, an assault that was very likely an attempted murder went way beyond ugly. It was downright chilling. A random assault is heinous because the victim often did nothing more than be at the wrong place at the wrong time and got the crap kicked out him or her because of it. A targeted assault raises a whole different set of questions. Questions about the attacker, the motive and the modus. Questions about the victim, most specifically why he or she was targeted in the first place. In this case, a specifically targeted sexual assault, the questions were multiplying like fruit flies on a rotting peach, all of them disgusting.

Bishop was well known and respected in the community and, it turns out, a closeted bisexual or homosexual. He was a man who made a very bad choice, sneaked out for a couple of hours of forbidden pleasure on Christmas Eve and damn near got himself killed for it. Officially, they'd so far managed to keep his name out of the news, citing "pending notification of next of kin." But Plymouth is a small town, and by the time Fitz was on his way to South Point General, the victim's name and the circumstances of the assault were out on the streets, his reputation was in ruins and his family shattered, not only by what had been done to Winslow Bishop, but by the circumstances that led to its happening.

Fitz had nothing against people living alternative lifestyles. God knows there were enough of them, several in his own family, in fact. What saddened him beyond measure was that in this day and age, people still felt they needed to deny it or hide it away because of the possibly still unspeakable consequences of coming out.

Fitz signaled for a right and pulled into the hospital parking lot and thought about what the next hour was going to be like. There was no way the interview was going to be anything but invasive and disturbing. However you cut it, stripping away years and layers of protective coloration and leaving a person exposed for all to see was a nasty business.

But asking the tough questions, and asking them again and again, was how he found the baddies and got them off the street. If the victim's assailant was, in fact, the three-time LBGTQ serial killer who'd missed his mark on Christmas Eve, there was no doubt that it was only a matter of time before he struck again. Fitz turned off the engine and quick-stepped through the frigid air to the main entrance. He could feel the inside heat coming around the edges of the revolving door. He looked down at his watch, stepped into one of the moving glass enclosures and leaped out into the marble foyer. Jaysus, he hated these things.

Timing was a big player in any criminal investigation, and Fitz had none to waste. Memories fade, victims evade, and the perps lay low until, like a coiled cobra, they strike again.

34

Fitz identified himself and the patient he wanted to see to Nurse Cantrell at the ICU desk. He then followed the directions to the numbered glass cubicle where Winslow Bishop, a massive bandage on his head and a thick foam collar restricting his movements, was looking decidedly better than the other night. The TV, tuned to a movie channel, was hanging onto the wall like a malevolent insect, and the tray table holding the remains of a liquid lunch had been pushed to one side but was still within reach. Fitz stayed standing outside the cubicle and waited until the man looked up and made eye contact. When he did, he winced and tried to look away but was prevented from doing so by the bandage and the collar. He looked trapped and frightened and, finally, resigned.

"May I come in?"

Bishop responded with an almost imperceptible affirmative nod, followed by a sharp intake of breath. Moving hurt.

Fitz introduced himself and explained that he was the detective assigned to his case, and as such, he hoped he could stay and ask a few questions about what happened.

"Whatever," Bishop whispered. "Can't talk much. Hurts."

"I'll bet it does. The man who did this to you tried to kill you. You might not think so right now, but you got lucky. You were stronger than he bargained for."

Bishop snorted in muffled disgust. "I'm finished, you know." A pause for breath. "Wife, kids, job. Gone! How could I have been so fucking stupid?" Tears were rolling unchecked out of his eyes. Fitz held up a tissue, got a nodded permission and gently blotted up the moisture seeping out from under the white wrappings.

"Thanks."

"Look, Mr. Bishop, there is just no easy way around this, and I'm sorry for that. If we are going to find the man who did this to you and prevent him from attacking and possibly killing someone else, I'm going to have to ask you some really personal questions. You have the right to refuse to answer me, but if we don't do it here in private, I will have to bring you in for questioning the minute you're mobile, even if it means rolling you out of here in a chair."

"I can walk. They make me." He made a futile gesture with his unwired arm. "Go ahead and ask. I've got nothing left to lose. Not anymore."

Fitz had to work hard to hear the man through the bandages, but he was managing to do it. "Don't be so sure of that, sir. Right now it feels like the end of everything, but you're still alive, man, and that's something. You almost weren't. If you're alive, it means you have a future, and if you believe that you have a future, you have hope. Last question before we start: may I have your permission to tape this interview?"

A weak dispirited nod.

Fitz pulled a visitor chair over to the side of the bed and took out a tiny digital recorder, a pocket-sized note pad and a No. 2 yellow pencil.

35

Viridienne was fidgety. Restless. Out of sorts. Part of the problem was that she had time on her hands, and she wasn't used to it. She was between projects and commissions, she'd finished and delivered her Christmas orders, and she wasn't particularly inspired to start something new. She'd watched any number of old movies, still a delicious treat after a cinema-deprived childhood, and was feeling temporarily overdosed and bleary eyed. Emily had gone out for coffee with a friend, and Fitz was investigating the Christmas Eve attack that the media was now describing as both a hate crime and a sexual assault. She didn't know the victim personally, but there are no secrets in a small town. Not for very long, anyway.

Everyone in town knew of the family. Bishop was well-heeled Mayflower descendant, and until the night of the attack, he had been well hidden in the closet. She amended that thought. Somebody knew. Merry Christmas! Thinking about the ironic sadness of it all was not helping. There was nothing on earth she could do about it. On the other hand, perhaps she could. One never knows. She was actually drumming her finger tips on the edge of the chair, wondering which loose thread she might pick up and not finding any.

When all else fails, check your email. Good idea!

She pocketed her phone and started upstairs with the intention of ensconcing herself in her bedroom, checking her email, cruising around on Facebook, and after that playing a few hundred games of computer solitaire. But halfway up she stopped and reversed direction. If Kevin Daly was coming sooner rather than later, the least she could do for the man was freshen up his room. She'd do a quick once-over with a broom and a dust-cloth, push open the windows for a couple of minutes and get some fresh air in there and wipe down the fixtures in the bathroom he'd be using.

What she really wanted to do was to go into his room and have a little snoop around when no one was looking, but that went against everything she believed in. "Thou shalt not pry into other people's business, or into their diary, or into the top drawer of someone else's nightstand." It was one of her own personal commandments, especially as the owner and manager of a newly established B&B. However, as that same owner and manager, she had every right, indeed a moral and professional duty, to go in there before the man actually settled in and make sure everything was up to standard. Didn't she?

Of course, she did.

Thus rationalized, and with the matter now settled in her mind, she grabbed a dust rag and a broom out of the utility closet and walked down the narrow hallway to the

Bradford Room, now Kevin Daly's room. She was a woman on a mission with a recently cleared conscience.

Viridienne was surprised to find his door locked. It made her briefly curious but only briefly. Some people are door lockers, some are not. He'd get over it once they all settled in and he felt more at home with everyone. Or maybe he wouldn't. Each to his own. He was a paying customer, not a blood relative. The man could lock a door if he wanted to.

Using her master key, she unlocked the door and stepped inside. It smelled closed up, but other than its being stuffy, everything appeared to be in order. The boxes that Fitz had helped to carry in were stacked at the end of the bed in almost military order. A row of three stacks of three, identically sized, brand-new cardboard boxes. Nine boxes in all. Carefully placed. Securely taped. She turned away and opened the clothes closet.

Kevin's clothing was still in the zippered garment bags. Three of them. The bags themselves were hanging, spaced evenly apart from one another, on the closet rail. On the shelf above the hanging pole, she could see the stack of clean towels, the extra blanket and pillow and the small table top ironing board and travel iron she left in each room for the use of the guests.

As a matter of personal prerogative, Viridienne did not have Bibles in the rooms. Her thinking was, if somebody really needed one, they could get it on line. And that's what she told the representative from the Gideon Society when he contacted her.

She pushed the closet door shut and opened the one window as high as it would go, counted to sixty and pulled it shut. Just enough fresh air to give the space a thorough, very cold and very brief, airing out.

That's better!

After a quick wipe down with a dust rag and a couple of swipes with a hand-made broom she'd got at a local craft fair, one she swapped for one of her weavings, the bedroom was suitably refreshed. Inside the bathroom, she straightened the towels and didn't bother to wonder how they got out of line.

Then she put the little triangle motel-fold back on the end of the toilet paper. She thought she'd already done that, as well, but realized that between the time that Kevin had dropped off his things and today, it was not unreasonable to think that either Fitz or Em had gone in there and used it. There was no outside window in this tiny room, just a shower, a sink and a toilet. There was just enough room to turn around without banging your elbows. It was a retrofit in the house's architectural history. It was "cozy" and therefore quick and easy to clean and was still fully functional. That's really all that mattered, and because of her efforts, it was picture perfect and spotless.

Now she felt better. Now she could go play solitaire without a shred of guilt. But after all that work, she was hungry. If it isn't one damn thing, it's another, she thought, and then smiled as she pictured the remains of the Christmas cake swaddled in aluminum foil and lying in the refrigerator.

Life is good, she thought, walking through the dining room and out toward the kitchen. And life is even better when you're built like a stork and can eat anything you want, whenever you want, and never gain an ounce. Emily and Fitz both envied her this. Emily was simply of a softer rounder build. Certainly not fat, but in time she could go there. Fitz was built like a small ox. He worked out and lifted weights and was, for his almost average height, as strong as the ox he resembled.

Yes, she thought with a contented sigh, life is most definitely good. It was time for some of that cake and a cup of fresh coffee.

36

T he man with the computer and the bloody hands was in hiding. He was holed up in the next town, staying in a multi-storied, low-priced motel directly off the highway that advertised itself as being family and pet friendly. Under ordinary circumstances it would have been his last choice, but he needed anonymity. People in budget motels with pets and kids to look after are not as observant, demanding or critical as someone staying in a Hilton or a Marriott.

During the day he would continue with his regular comings and goings the way he had done before Christmas Eve. Nothing to raise even a flicker of suspicion. Staying locked up in the room and never going out would look weird. People booked into motels so they could sleep and shower in one place, but during the day they were out tourist-ing or visiting or doing business. He made sure he didn't look any different from the others. On the outside.

On the inside he was more distraught and agitated than he had ever been in his life. No, there had been one other time. He shook his head and pushed the shameful memory back under the rock where it mostly stayed. He had work to do, and he didn't need any more distraction. He had some serious thinking to do before moving on. The failed operation of the other night had thrown him off his stride. Badly. At issue was whether to stay and finish up with the third man he was grooming or abort the whole thing and get out of town. Wisdom said, cut bait and run. His obsession with order and the number three said, you have to do everything in threes. It was one of the rules. You have to finish what you start was another one. If you don't finish what you start, something awful will happen, and he couldn't ever risk that.

Reason told him after one slip-up, there is often another. Was he getting old and losing his touch, or was this a one-off? Who could have known the guy was a ninja warrior? And what would he tell the police? The man did know that his cover and his internet persona were virtually uncrackable. He'd spent a long time doing professional undercover work earlier in his life and knew all about creating and juggling multiples identities and keeping each and every one of them busy and under the radar. All those little alter egos running around working for him, making him good money, and then on Christmas Eve, he blew it. Literally. Damn!

The good news is that he was okay for money. Currently he had three women on his phishing lines, his usual number, and he was slowly and expertly reeling them in. It was convenient that he could phish from anywhere. All he needed was a computer and a post office box number. He snorted in disgust. The women that he hooked were so desperate for attention and love and so willing to believe anything he told them. They threw themselves headlong into his outspread net while he methodically showered them with compliments, wrote long flowery letters, sent anonymous bouquets of day-old flowers and made-in-China trinkets, made false promises … and just as methodically emptied their bank accounts.

To a woman, they were so understanding and forgiving, so willing to accept the endless and inevitable work-related demands and changes in his schedule that always at the last minute prevented his finally coming to see them in person, even though they'd already sent the money for the nonrefundable plane ticket, the hotel and, of course, the car rental. This will never happen again; he would promise them all. But of course, it always did. That's how he made his money.

After a cancelled visit, he would write, "Don't worry, my darling, I'm so sorry, but it's only money. I'll get it back to you, you know that. Remember, my money is locked up over here. There will be a next time, I promise. I'll make it happen. I can't live without you. Please tell me you'll wait for me? Signed with sad-faced emoji.

He would always follow one of these up with surprise bouquet of a flowers or a special delivery teddy bear. Both were equally effective.

The man needed a different plan for here and now. As he saw it, he had two options. If he stayed with Plan A and went to the place he'd booked into, he could lay low and operate out of there. That way, he'd be hiding out in the open, right under everybody's noses. Not something your average killer does. He liked that idea. And with that eager little police detective, Fitz-what's-his-name, hanging around all the time, no one on God's green earth would ever think to look for him there. It was the perfect cover. Talk about camouflage and protective coloration all rolled up into one. That, and he liked the cat. Even if it was a bit stand-offish.

Plan B would be to give his regrets to Viridienne, offer her half of the full amount to cancel the rental agreement, drop off the hired car, get the hell out of town on the next train and set up shop somewhere else.

But that would cancel plans for his third target. That, plus the fact that he hadn't finished what he'd set out to do with Winslow Bishop, a name he'd only learned when he heard about the assault in the paper and later read it in the local paper. So in reality there was no Plan B, but he still had to make a choice. He could get himself some hospital scrubs at a local thrift shop or a Walmart, sneak into the hospital and finish the job. Or he could cut this one loose and move on to his third target, treat him as his number two, and find himself a new number three. If he went that route, he'd have to work fast to stay within his three-month timeframe, but he didn't see this as a problem. There was no lack of "men seeking men" for a discreet breathless and anonymous encounter. The more he thought about it, the more finding a new hit seemed the easiest and the most sensible, and there's no time like the present.

That's better, he thought, pushing back from what passed for a desk in the one-size-fits-all motel room. First, a shower, then out and get himself a drive-through lunch. After that a little shopping trip and … but at the incoming mail ding from his computer, he put it all on hold, dropped back into the chair and looked at his screen.

Business before pleasure or, with a little bit of luck, maybe both. He could hear the dog in the next room barking. It irritated him. He hit enter, and a familiar image flashed onto the screen.

"Hi there, Mystery Man…you say you want discretion? I know

all about discretion. It's my middle name. There are advantages to staying in the closet, and I know every eye-watering and heart-thumping one of them from personal experience. I live on the south shore, and let's just say I know my way around in more ways than one."

HE WAS TRYING to come up with an enticing response but was distracted by the dog barking in the unit next door. Part of him wanted to pound on the wall in frustration, but that might cause someone to take notice of him and then remember him. He stuffed wet Kleenex in his ears and hunkered down. Might as well make himself a little money first, then he'd go have some lunch.

"HELLO AGAIN, my darling. Just thinking about writing to you makes my fingers and everything else tingle with excitement. You have no idea how knowing you has changed my life and lifted me out of the depression that darkens my days...AND MY NIGHTS. You have given me something to look forward to again. I have good news. I think the higher ups are going to turn me loose for a couple of days. You know, time off for good behavior? Hahahaha. Sadly, not enough time to get all the way to the states, but certainly enough to meet you halfway, say in Paris? How does a weekend in the city of lights sound to you? I'll start making the arrangements the minute I know you will be able to join me. By the way, you know I hate asking, but I might need a little help up front getting my ticket and booking the hotel. I'll bring enough cash with me so I can pay you back before we do ...anything else! Love, always, M"

AND THEN...

"Dearest Marietta, I'm counting the days until I'm a free man. I have you to thank for this, you know. Until we started writing, I had no reason to better myself. Now I do. As I understand it they are going to move me to transitional housing, and when they do, I'll be able to get a job and be the man who can provide a life for you. Can you believe this? Tell me you are ready to move on to the next chapter, and I'll let you know what I am going to need. But for now, we need to keep this precious little secret as ours alone. Not a word to anyone else, OK, my love?

Yours, soon to be forever, Mark"

THE TIME-STAMP on his computer signaled it was time for lunch.

37

Seated at the kitchen table with an empty plate in front of her and DT curled on a chair next to her, Viridienne was considering a second slice of cake but stopped herself mid-reach, not out of concern for her waistline, but out of consideration for her sister and hopefully for Fitz, both of whom would certainly come in later on looking for leftovers.

Now that she thought about it, she wasn't so sure about Fitz coming by. She knew he was deeply involved in work right now. The murder on South Point and the murderous attack on Burial Hill were taking up a lot of everyone's time. He never said the two were related, but the newspapers and cable news were making that assumption, and Viridienne herself would have to be completely oblivious to what was going on in town not to put the two together and come up with the obvious. But what did it mean, and how were they related? She'd never learn it from Fitz.

She smiled at the thought of him. He was almost six inches shorter than she, several years younger and built like a fire plug—not fat, just solid. She suspected that his just under average height was, or once had been, an issue for him that he may have compensated for by constantly pushing himself to the limit. He lifted weights and studied the martial arts, and just to keep everything in balance, he wrote poetry. Beautiful, sensitive, thoughtful poetry. A multi-faceted individual, to be sure, and one she was growing increasingly fond of. He had given her every reason to trust him. He never once overstepped a boundary. Even now, with recent access to her bed, keys to her house and a special friend ring on her finger, he maintained an open and respectful distance as they moved slowly and carefully closer to one another.

The sweet reverie was pleasantly interrupted by the sound of the front door opening and Emily's cheery voice calling out, "Hey, Vid, I'm home. You in the kitchen?"

"Yes, I'm in the kitchen, and if you get in here fast enough, I won't eat your piece of cake."

"Fitz coming over tonight?" Emily was dishing herself up a piece of cake. "Any hot coffee left in the pot? I'm freezing."

"To your first question, I have no idea. He's really involved in this murder case, meaning he's super busy. He hasn't called in yet, and he always calls before he comes over. I guess that's a long way around of saying I don't know. To your second question, about the coffee? I just made some. Help yourself."

Emily did just that and then seated herself across the table from her sister.

"Vid?"

"Mm?"

"What's it like having a boyfriend?" She stopped, held up her hand and amended the question. "Whoa, I don't mean the personal stuff. I mean, like, you know, having a *boyfriend?* I mean what's it like having a regular someone to go places with, someone who calls you up just because he likes to hear the sound of your voice?"

Viridienne cocked her head and favored her sister with a questioning look. "Are you trying to tell me something?"

"Maybe?"

"Let me get myself some more coffee, okay? Then, if you want to, tell me what's happening."

While she was refilling her cup, Viridienne carved off another sliver of the remains of the Christmas cake but carefully left one last slice for Fitz … if the man didn't wait too long before coming by to claim it.

"Now, then, are you saying that someone's caught your eye?"

"Well, not exactly. I mean yes and not yet, sort of."

Viridienne tipped her head to one side and looked at her sister. "Emily Rose, finding a person who cares for you, and someone you care for as well, is really nice. It took me long enough. It was the last thing I was looking for when Rose died. But here comes this police detective. He's the man who found the monster that killed my best friend. He's the man who, when it was all over, didn't hit on me the minute the case was closed. A man who took his time to get to know me, and now a man that I've discovered I like to spend time with."

"Do you think you'll ever get married?"

Viridienne shook her head. "To be honest, I haven't given it a whole lot of thought. Certainly not right now or any time soon, if ever, for that matter. Now that I am thinking about it, I don't see any reason why I, or we, should. I don't want kids. I own my own home. I like my work, and I can do it for as long as I can lift my arms over my head," she chuckled, "and remember what I was doing when I raised them." She paused and looked across the table at her sister. "But this is not about me. Are you saying you've found, as they say these days, a person of interest? Who is he, and what's he like?"

Emily chewed on the corner of her lip before saying, "I, uh, met him online."

Viridienne's eyebrows shot all the way up to her hairline.

"You've met some guy on the internet?"

Emily nodded. "It's a site called You-Me-We. The first month was free. I met a couple of guys, actually. Well, a couple of guys answered my ad. But this one seemed kind of interesting. We haven't actually met yet, so I'm not really going out with him."

"You put in an ad online? You put your information out there for anyone to see?" Viridienne was trying not to shout, but despite her best efforts her voice was rising. "How long has this been going on?"

"Viridienne, calm down. I got the idea from my friends at the college. We don't do bars, we're too old for a church youth group, and the guys in our classes are all nerds. Do you realize that since I've been out of the Society I've never been out on a date?"

"That's my point, Em. Don't take me wrong now. You think you are all grown up, but in a lot of ways you are more like twelve or thirteen, innocent and inexperienced. There are some real creeps out there trolling the internet, looking for fresh meat. Take your time There's no rush. You have no idea what you're doing in that department. At least, not yet."

"Not true, Vid. I'm very good with computers. You know that. Before I escaped from the Believers, they let me work in the office. What they didn't know was I learned my way around a whole lot more than just spreadsheets and online record keeping. Then, when I did get out, and that lovely family rescued me, they showed me how to use the social internet to find you. That wasn't all bad now, was it? It took me a while, but I didn't give up." She paused and looked at her older sister. "And neither did you."

Viridienne's voice was rising. "That's not the point, Em. You've lived most of your life in a cage, inside a shell, inside a concentration camp. I know, I was in there, too. It took me years to stop looking over my shoulder and flinching if a man came anywhere near me."

"I'm not you, Viridienne."

Viridienne exhaled, dropped her shoulders and sat back in her chair. "You're right, Em. Sorry for the lecture. I'm being the overprotective big sister. Let's go back to the beginning. Tell me about him." She paused. "Um, you did say guy as in male?"

"I did. His name is Joe Franklin. He's in the Navy right now, but he grew up on Cape Cod. North Falmouth. I looked it up on Google, it's not far from here. He said his family still lives there."

"What does he do for work in the Navy, and where is he stationed?"

"He's a medic on a ship. He's planning on going into the medical field when he gets out, as either a nurse or a physician's assistant."

"So you haven't met him in person yet."

Emily shook her head. "Not yet. Soon, though, he's got leave coming up in February."

"Have you Googled his name and/or his parents' names yet?"

Another head shake.

"Do you have a picture of him?

She brightened, "I do. He's cute. I'll go get my computer and show you."

"Can't you pull it up on your phone?"

"Phone's too small. We can get a bigger image on the computer." Her eyes were dancing now, her growing excitement evident.

"Go on, then. Now I can't wait to meet him, so to speak."

Emily was back in a flash and positioned her open laptop on the table between them. She tapped in a code, and in seconds the engaging clear-eyed face of young man in uniform came up on the screen. "Viridienne, meet Joe."

Viridienne extended a hand towards the computer and wiggled her fingers. "Pleased to meet you, Joe. He's good looking. I'll give you that."

Emily gave her sister a playful smack on the shoulder and said, "See, I told you."

"Okay, so, he's in the navy, his parents live on the Cape, he's coming home in February. Have you Skyped or Face-timed with him yet?"

Emily chewed on her lower lip. "No. I guess I wanted to tell you about him before I did. But he can't do that right now anyway."

"Why not? If he can send emails and go on a match-making site, he can certainly Skype. That doesn't make sense."

"I asked, but he said it was something about ship security They can send words but not pictures. Heck, I'd like to see what the ship looks like. I asked, but he said it wasn't allowed for security reasons. He can't even give me the name of the ship."

Viridienne did not ask how he managed to get his

picture up on the dating site, but there was no doubt she would. Right now, she didn't want to stop the bubbling flow of information, and open skepticism would do just that.

"So it's all been email and jpgs so far."

She nodded. "We've only been writing back and forth for a couple of weeks. I wanted to get to know him better. We're still using the dating site email. My girlfriends at school said, 'Only use your first name, or just your initials if you want to be super careful. Never give out your real information, like your home address, where you work, or your email or phone number, until you have met them in person.'"

"Did they tell you all that? It's good advice. What else did they say?"

"Always have that first date in a very public, well lighted place. Park your own car out of sight so he can't get your license number, and never get into a car with him."

"All good advice, but…"

They were interrupted by the sound of an incoming text on Viridienne's phone. It was from Kevin Daly.

"Hello there, Viridienne, if it's all right with you and your sister…and of course, the cat, I'd like to settle in the day after tomorrow. I know I have a key, and you can call me old-fashioned, but it just feels better to have you there when I officially move in. Please let me know if this works for you. Cordially, Kevin."

SHE TAPPED OUT A RESPONSE.

"HI, Kevin, any time after two in the afternoon is fine.

We'll all be home by then, and the welcome mat will be out on the front porch. See you tomorrow. V."

"WHAT WAS THAT?"

"Kevin Daly is moving in tomorrow."

"You don't look exactly thrilled."

"I'm not un-thrilled. It's just going to be a change, that's all, and life is change, is it not? I'll adjust. But backing up to where we were before the text came in. If you're not using your own name on the dating site, what name are you using?"

"Emmaline Greene."

Viridienne chuckled despite her anxiety. "Well, that's one way of keeping it in the family, isn't it?"

38

Fitz was seated at his desk, reviewing the file on the South Point murder case, when his partner breezed in, smelling like cold fresh air.

"Hey, thanks for coming in, Alison. I know you wanted this week at home with the kids. I never would have asked, but I really need to run all this by someone who knows the drill before I take it any further. I owe you one."

"This coffee for me?" She reached for the paper cup before waiting for an answer. "It's still freezing out there. I'll be glad when this cold snap breaks, and we can get it all the way up to twenty degrees out there. And you don't owe me anything. So what did you find out?"

"A lot! First thing this morning, a homeless guy shows up at my office door with a package he dug out of a dumpster, bloody clothing and rubber gloves. He saw some guy stuffing it in there in the wee hours of Christmas morning and got curious. Forensics have it right now."

"Jesus."

"You might say that. I fed the guy, offered him a shower

and some clean clothes out of the emergency closet. Then I gave him forty of my own dollars and told him if he heard or saw anything that might be of interest to please call me. After that I went to the hospital to see what I could learn from the victim."

"And?" She was making short, grateful work of her coffee.

"I called you on the way back. There's a lot to process, and I need you to help me sort through it. He let me tape the interview."

"You got lucky."

In more ways than one, thought Fitz, but he kept the second reason he got lucky to himself. Let her wonder what his little half-smile was about.

"What did the victim say? No, I take that back. Start at the beginning. Tell me how badly he was injured and how he's doing now, then you can move on to the information we have to work with."

"It's not nice. He's pretty beat up. The attacker tried to strangle him from behind, but he wasn't prepared for the strength and the quick reflexes of his victim. When the guy started screaming, he slammed the man's head into a grave-stone to shut him up and took off running. That's when and where the drunk partygoers came along and called 911. Good thing they did. In that cold and with those injuries, the poor bugger wouldn't have lasted very long."

Alison shook her head in sympathy, drained the last of her coffee and chucked the empty container in the direction of the wastebasket, scoring a direct hit.

Fitz continued. "I questioned the guys that found him, but they couldn't tell us much. We did collect blood and skin from the gravestone. Forensics will tell us whether they match the victim's blood and skin or if there's anything in all of it that might be from the attacker. Would that ever be a bonus. I don't know how he managed it, but this guy has never left one molecule of his DNA anywhere."

"We might get lucky this time. This guy fought back. There's gonna be something somewhere. There has to be."

"Let's hope so. There are definite parallels to the South Point murder. Bishop met his attacker online, had a first date with him that went well, and then agreed to hook up again the other night. If you ask me, which you're not, I'd say it's not exactly the most salubrious way to spend your time on Christmas Eve."

"He took one hell of a chance."

Fitz nodded. "No accounting. Desperation, lust, the thrill of a secret encounter, who knows. Bad things like that don't happen in Plymouth? Whatever it was, he damn near got himself killed for it, and he certainly would have been, had he not been as fast and fit as he was and there weren't a couple of good-hearted drunk revelers within earshot. Mr. Perfect Crime didn't account for that. Maybe he's beginning to slip."

"Creepy."

"Bishop told me that when he regained consciousness, he tried to look up the guy on his phone, but the account had been shut down. Still, we have his side of the conversation."

Alison brightened. "We can still get stuff the average person can't. We just need to get hold of the device. It's evidence."

"I tried. He wouldn't give it up. I decided not to arm-wrestle him for it. At least not then."

"He will, though, or we'll confiscate it as evidence."

"The man's not thinking straight. The worst part of it, if there is any way for it to get worse, is that he's completely shattered by being out-ed in such a degrading way. Right now, his life is in ruins. His wife is furious, hurt, shamed, outraged, screaming for a divorce and says he can't come home. The kids—teens, a boy and a girl—are a mess. It's bad enough that their dad was mugged and almost killed, but the how and why of it, the circumstances and the media coverage have really done a number on them. You know how vicious kids can be. I almost feel worst for the kids. That's a long way around of saying, we'll get the phone."

"What was the MO?"

"Pretty typical of this kind of thing. Men-seeking-men site. One of the back-channel ones. They keep changing names. Frequented mostly by guys in the closet or guys who want to stray from hubby and don't want to get caught or guys looking for kinky. Let's just say, you don't want to know any more."

Alison winced.

"Anyway, it seems that he'd been on one of those sites on and off for a couple of years. Never had a problem. He always had a coffee or a drink-date with a new guy first and checked them out. Then he'd go for a second, maybe a third date, and then over and out. Back into the void until the urge became unquenchable. It's sad."

"It's human and sad. Both together."

"Now what?" said Alison.

"Comparing it to the South Point case, that man was not in the closet. He was married to another guy and just wanted a little quick action on the side. From what we've learned so far, this guy Bishop was deeply in the closet but desperate. He'd done this kind of thing, once or twice before. Back channel internet search. They start emailing using fake names, arrange to hook up, have sex and never see each other again. Over and out."

Fitz held out his hand, thumb and forefinger extended, to emphasize his points.

"This one started out the same way only…well you don't need all the details. The murderer strangles him from behind. The victim literally never sees it coming. In the case of the South Point murder, we think the encounter and the murder happened somewhere else, and the perp moved the body to the location where he dumped it. Trouble is, the tide wasn't high enough that day, and the body got stuck in the rocks. Clearly the perp's not from around here."

She looked curious. "Why do you say that."

He gave her a pained look. "Alison, Plymouth is on the coast. Half the residents here own boats for their fishing and the other half fish directly off the beach. There isn't anyone from this town who doesn't live by the tides, either directly or indirectly. A local would have checked a tide chart before he dumped something heavy off the bluff."

"Fair point. Now what?"

"We go into the national databank, look through the other cases for what else we can find and see if we can construct a pattern. So far, we know the victims are all gay or bisexual men, the murders happen in threes a couple of weeks apart. The victims were all strangled from behind following a sexual encounter." He shook his head and held up his hand. "Don't ask. It's not pretty. We've had no DNA samples until now, and so the perp has been completely untraceable.

"It seems that close friends and relatives of the victims had no idea that the murdered men were having a secret relationship. Finally, when the forensic people went through the computers and the cell phones of the victims, any evidence of who he might have been communicating with was gone."

"I didn't think you could do that, erase everything without a trace."

"You can't. The average person can't. It takes a very computer savvy, very meticulous, detail oriented individual to retrieve erased or scrubbed data, someone with a lot of practice at staying well under the radar. They're out there, Alison, but by the very nature of what they do and how they operate, we are never likely to meet them in broad daylight. If we do, we'll never know. You know as well as I do, some of the worst criminals on record were described by people who knew them casually as great neighbors, good to animals, yadda, yadda, yadda." He made a circling motion with his hand.

"I repeat, creepy."

"But this time it looks like we've got a chance. We have a victim that lived, a victim I haven't finished questioning. The big thing is, eventually we'll get his phone with all the conversations on it. We may not have the perp's name, but people write in signature word groupings and patterns. It's a lot like how musicians use certain riffs and the same timing sequences repeatedly. Well, people who write do the same thing. I'm going to look at the emails and then go on the site and see if I can find the pattern."

"Jesus, Fitz, you're sounding more like a professor than a detective. Where did you learn so much about writing?"

"Did you forget I have an M.A. in Irish Literature and Poetry? Along with that comes a lot of practice in recognizing and identifying writing quirks, sentence formulae and rhythms and individual flourishes."

She clapped her hand to her forehead. "And with all that book-learning, here you are, a cop." She shook her head in mock disbelief.

"I'm the very bane of my sainted mother's existence."

This was punctuated with an exaggerated eye-roll. "She wanted me to be an academic like herself, ivied halls and all that. To be honest, I couldn't bear the thought of it. I like reading poetry, and I like writing it; but the thought of teaching it day in and day out makes my skin crawl."

"You are too much, Fitzy-Fitz. I pulled you off topic. Let's get back to sex, drugs, rock and roll and attempted murder."

He responded with a short bark of a laugh. "Right. Next steps. I'm going back tomorrow morning and have an extended visit with Winslow Bishop. I want to sit down and go over the whole thread line by line. Then, when I know what I'm doing, I'll give myself a sexy name, go to that very site, lay out some bait and see what I can reel in."

"You're going to try and set up a sting operation?"

"The very self-same thing, my dear."

"You're playing with fire, you know."

"It's why we get the big bucks. Besides, you don't ever go into a sting alone. I'll have plenty of backup, and we know the guy doesn't use a gun."

"I can't really see you creating that kind of persona and making it believable. You're too nice."

"There's another thing I didn't tell you. I minored in theater at Trinity." He struck a theatrical pose and pointed at the window. "Lo, what light through yonder window breaks? It is the east, and Juliet is the sun … and so forth."

Allison was laughing out loud now. "You are also, in two words, too much."

Fitz stepped back into his detective skin, "Another thing. For the first time ever, we have witnesses. We have those three guys who saw the attacker take off. They didn't get a good look, but they got a look, and they called 911. That may have saved the guy's life. We'll have even more to go on when we get the forensics report. What with it being the week between Christmas and New Year, we aren't running on all fourteen cylinders. Lots of people taking a little time off."

She covered her face. "And I'm one of the no-shows."

He waved it away. "Alison, I know you wanted the time off, and God knows you deserve it, but could you manage give me a couple of hours here and there if I need it? Maybe even talk on the phone."

"I can do that. We're a team, remember."

39

"**M**r. Bishop. Winslow, are you awake? Open your eyes. Your wife Ginger is here to see you." Nurse manager Cindy Cantrell spoke gently but loudly enough to be heard.

Bishop opened his eyes and quickly turned his head away and shut them. With visible effort he croaked, "I'll sign anything, give you everything, apologize to everyone, get out of town and get out of your life for good. I'll just disappear."

"He's been coming in and out for the last few hours," Cindy told Ginger. "But he is awake now. Ring if you need me, I'll be at my desk," she pointed, "right there, if you need me."

"Winn."

He opened his eyes and held up his hand to stop her from saying anything more. "Ginger, I am so goddamn sorry. You have no idea. You and the kids didn't deserve this. I've wrecked everything we've worked for and … and … well, I wish I *had* died the other night."

"Don't talk like that," she snapped. "I know you probably don't believe me right now, but I still love you."

He stopped for breath and then sobbed, "I never stopped. I just …"

Now it was his wife's turn to halt the conversation. "Just be quiet, will you? The reality is, you didn't die. You may not believe this either, but I'm thankful to God you didn't. Am I furious, humiliated, outraged, and if you weren't already such a bloody mess, would I like to land a good one on the other side of your head? Yes! Will I do it? No."

"But …"

"Look, Winn, will you just stop trying to talk and listen to me? I didn't finish. I don't want you dead, and I don't want you gone, but I also don't know of any way forward right now. I'm willing to try and see if there is one. Just give me some time. Meanwhile, I came in to find out if you needed anything from the house. They told me they are going to move you out of intensive care and down to critical care, and if you keep improving, you might be able to get out by the end of the week."

Her husband raised both hands, wordlessly asking the obvious question, where?

"Your mother and your sister have both called and offered."

He covered his bandaged face with both hands and groaned in raw anguish. "Oh God, they know?

"Winn, everybody knows."

Bishop covered his face with his hands. Ginger leaned forward and pulled them away from his face and looked him straight in the eye.

"Winn, you didn't kill anyone, and you didn't commit a crime. You made one hell of a mistake and damn near got yourself killed for it. Meanwhile, we are still married; we have two kids, and you are still their father. We own a house, and your name's still on the mortgage. We have four living parents, and each of us has siblings. You can't walk away from all of this. I won't let you."

"But...how...?"

She paused, still holding onto his hands, "I just need time, Winn. We all do. We'll find a way forward. I can't imagine what that's going to be yet, but we're going to find it."

40

Viridienne tapped a message into her phone.

"Hey, Fitz. Kevin Daly just texted me to say he'll be moving in tomorrow afternoon. Just thought I'd let you know. V"

"Hi V, on a case right now. Can I come by later on and beg a cup of tea from you when I get off work this afternoon? We can talk about it then. Not sure when. Will text when I know."

"Yes, but you'd better hurry. That last piece of Christmas cake is looking pretty good, and there's no one here to defend it."

"Don't you dare. TTLY" <3

Viridienne texted a "😊!" back and pocketed her phone. She was deeply troubled by the thought that her sister might be looking for love in all the wrong places. She knew she was not her sister's keeper, but that didn't stop her from worrying. She couldn't run interference for everything that came her way, nor could she protect her from the slings and arrows of the life she'd willingly come into after leaving the cult. But Viridienne was creative and resourceful, not to mention determined. Didn't she help find the man that killed the woman who willed her the very house she was standing in? Of course, she almost got herself killed in the process, but she preferred not to think about that part.

But it was Fitz who'd come to her rescue. She had been back in her little cottage by the pond, desperately stalling for time with a would-be killer standing directly in front of her, when she figured out a way to get a text message to him. She considered it to be one of her finer, as well as scariest, moments. Yes, Viridienne was resourceful. A force to be reckoned with. No one was going to get at her little sister without going through her first.

She went upstairs to her office-bedroom, which, with the recent exception of a recently invited guest, was her private sanctuary. Her *sanctum sanctorum*. She smiled, powered up her laptop and tapped in, "You-Me-We," and logged as a guest. This was uncharted territory. She'd heard about these things but never had the inclination to explore one.

She clicked on the Women Seeking Men category to see if she could find her sister's profile; Emmaline Greene or the initials E.G. ought not to be too hard to find. On the other hand, did Em use that as her first posting name, or did she use a total alias, and if so, what might it be? At first click, up came a list of first names or initials followed by a short descriptive paragraph.

"H₁, I'm Sally B. I like outdoor activities, camping hiking kayaking. I'm a devout Christian, and I have four dogs. I believe God has chosen a mate for me. Are you the one? I'm in my early forties, never been married. I have a good job. I like travel, reading and going to church.

I'm looking for a good Christian man who shares my interests and is interested in a serious long-term relationship. I'm old fashioned. If you are honest, a gentleman, don't smoke, drink or gamble, then send me a message."

AND ANOTHER.

"HELLO, you dare-devil you. I'm in my thirties, weight proportionate to height, spell that average, and I'm a spunky redhead with a mind for adventure. I ride a Harley, I can dance on a table or solo as nature made me right on your lap or on your back porch. I like long distance road trips, and I can give back as good as I get. If you think you are man enough, then hit reply, and let's make the rubber hit the road."

Nothing looked even vaguely familiar. Viridienne would later learn there was a strict one-hundred-word limit for an introductory listing. She wondered what she might write if she were so inclined but was interrupted from any further consideration of the question by the sound of knocking on the front door. Fitz! She looked at her watch, yipped in dismay, leaped out of her chair, raced down the stairs and pulled open the door.

41

"You don't have to knock. You have a key."

"I have a key, and out of respect, I will always knock, ring the bell or text you from the front porch. That being said, if for some reason I thought it necessary to come in unannounced, I would do it in a heartbeat, and then you'd never hear me until I was standing next to you. One of the things I picked up at the Dojo. I can move like a cat, when called upon to do so. And speaking of same, hello, DT."

He reached down to give the happy-to-see-him animal a vigorous chin scratch. "Don't you worry now, fella, I'm not takin' over yer territory, I'm just lettin' ye know, I can be right cat-quiet-like meself, when I want ter."

Viridienne dipped her head and kissed the man, who happily returned the favor and even upped the ante. "Now then, woman, do you think a man who is fairly dyin' of thirst can get a cup of tea in this place? He stopped and clapped his hand to his forehead. "Brainstorm! How about

I go make tea for the two of us, and you can finish up whatever you are doing."

"I accept. And while we're at it—the tea, that is—I need to ask your advice about something."

Once they were seated at the table with full mugs in front of them and the last surviving slice of the bouche de Noel on a plate in front Fitz, he said, "So what's this advice that you're needing?"

"It's probably silly and me being overprotective, but I just found out that Emily seems to have gotten herself an on-line boyfriend. I don't know whether I should keep my mouth shut and just be happy for her or go up there and dump a glass of water on her computer." She paused. "What do you think?"

"Funny you should ask."

"Why do you say that?"

"Let's just say that I'm investigating something in that direction myself."

"You mean the murder case?"

He held up his hand and shook his head. "You know I can't talk about my work, even to you. And apropos of nothing, do you think we could have Christmas more than once a year? This cake is orgasmic. It's even better with age." He winked at her.

"I'm not going to respond to that other than saying you can leave any comments about age out of it, if you don't mind. But back to my question. I'm serious. I'm worried that she's liable to get herself into something she might not know how to get herself out of."

"That's always a risk, Vid. You can get hurt walking down the street, too. When we're little, they tell us never to talk to strangers, right? Nowadays we do it all the time—

and I mean all the time. If you're not careful, some of it can get pretty nasty."

"That's what I mean. I don't want her to get hurt."

"Of course you don't, but you can't run ahead of her all the time either. I think you should take comfort in the fact that she told you and keep the lines of communication open."

"She showed me his picture and even told me her on-line name."

"Good! She's doing all the right things. Show interest, but don't pry."

"Um, I already went onto the site to check it out. I'd just logged on when you knocked on the door."

"And?"

"Like I said, I'd just logged on, so nothing really. I had only got as far as the first page, women looking for men. It was hysterical. Made me start thinking what I might write if I ever went onto one of those sites."

That got his attention. "Did you now?"

She reached over and patted his free hand. "No worries, Detective. Considering the pleasure I take in present company, the idea is only a fragment, a scrap, a passing curiosity, pure research. Nothing more."

"Whew." He wiped his brow in mock relief. "But getting back to Emily. The young ones are all doing it these days, and to be honest, it's no riskier than meeting up with some guy you don't know at a bar and going for a walk around the block. He paused. "But since you've already gone onto the site ..." He stopped and held up his hand in the "stop" position, "and for God's sake, don't ever tell her you have. But if you go back on and you find something you don't like the looks of, call me in."

"Thanks, Fitz, I will. More tea?"

He smiled and held out his mug. "You say Daly is coming in tomorrow?"

She nodded.

"And?" He looked thoughtful.

"The money will certainly help. I really am okay with it, you know. He seems nice enough, and he'll come and go as he pleases. It's not like I have to entertain him or anything. He's also a total neatnick."

"How do you know that?"

"I went into his room the other day to spiff it up and air it out before he moved in. Everything he brought in with him was arranged in perfect order, lined up in threes, stacked in threes. Even the clothes in the closet. The stuff was still in the garment bags, but even those, it's like he measured the spaces between them."

"Hardly a fault, Vid. The last thing you want living here is a slob or a hoarder. The man travels light. I took note of that myself. He'll be okay, I think. Besides, as you may or may not have noticed, I am a regular feature here in the kitchen and elsewhere. The man is not going get too out-of-line with a police presence in the next room. Now that I think about it, with all the snooping you're doing, if you ever need a little pocket money, we just might have work for you down at headquarters."

She waved him away. "Not hardly. I'm busy enough with my art, my sister, the B&B and the cat. I don't need a side job."

The two were happily interrupted by Emily, slide-stepping across the kitchen toward the coffee maker. "Hey, Fitz, I thought I heard your voice down here. Has my sister been telling you all about my online boyfriend? Don't bother answering that, I can see by her shifty look that she has. Any of the coffee left? I'm a total addict, you know." She poured herself a cup, took a sip and made a face. "Ew, this needs heating up."

"Em ..." Viridienne did indeed look sheepish.

"It's okay, Vid. I did what you said. I checked him out online, and he checks out."

"Checks out how?" Fitz asked. "I'm afraid This Irishman feels a little out of the loop here."

Emily now had a cup of freshly microwaved coffee in front of her and was bubbling on. "I've been talking to this guy online, and I didn't tell Vid, because I thought she wouldn't approve." She paused for a swallow of coffee. "So today, I told her, even showed her his picture. To make a long story short, Vid told me to do a Google search and check him out, so I did. I looked up his family, and they are listed as living on the Cape. Amazing what you can do on a search site."

"What else did you learn?" asked Fitz in a cautionary tone.

"Nothing. I would have had to pay for anything else, so I stopped with that, but I think that's enough, don't you? I mean, it matches up with what he told me."

"I think you've done all the right things, Em, and it sounds okay. I realize lots of people meet up online these days, and most of the sites are reasonably safe. Just don't ever send him any money, no matter how nice he sounds, and don't ever give him any of your banking or credit card numbers. If he asks, tell him you'll get back to him and call me immediately."

Em hesitated for only a microsecond, before giving Fitz an exasperated look. "I may still be feeling my way around here, but I'd never fall for one of those schemes. I may have just come into the real world, but it wasn't yesterday."

"The women and men, by the way, who do get hooked

by these phishers, spelled p-h-i-s-h, never think they will either, but these people are slick. They could sell ice cubes to Eskimos. But from what you tell me, this guy sounds perfectly all right. I look forward to meeting him sometime. Are you sure he hasn't asked you for money?"

"You're acting like a big brother, you know."

"I've been called worse things, and I accept the duty and the pleasure." He gave her a little mock bow and turned his full attention to the last of bit of cake on his plate.

"Hey there, Mr. Discreet, you sound like my kind of guy. Can we just skip all that crap about quiet walks on the beach and cozy dinners by the fire and just get to the point, so to speak? Where and when? Your call."

O n the following day Winn Bishop was indeed moved down a notch to the critical care unit and into a single room, one with a door that closed and a window, overlooking the parking lot, that opened. Not a particularly inspiring view, but it was a window, and the light coming through it was clear and bright. The man was clearly on the road back, but because he was no longer in the direct line of sight of the main desk, and Fitz was afraid he might still be a target, he'd requested that a police guard be on duty 24/7 outside his door.

Fitz was also Bishop's first visitor of the day, and this time, the man didn't look away. He still had the look of a man beaten in body and in soul, but at least he was willing to make eye contact.

"Looks like you're on the mend. Are they giving you solid food yet?"

"Soft foods. I can swallow now." Bishop lifted his hand to his discolored neck. "The bastard did a number on me."

"I know. Do you mind if I pull up a chair?"

"Be my guest. Talking hurts like hell."

"I'm sorry to hear that, but I do have to ask some more questions. I have my recorder, so you won't have to repeat anything. Do I have your permission to use it?"

A fraction of a nod.

"I'll get straight to the point. The sooner you give us your phone and your computer and anything else you used to communicate with the man who tried to kill you, the better chance we have of catching him before he goes after someone else. Think about it, man. You could save a life. We'll get them either way."

"Phone's in the drawer. I kept a separate one, and I had it with me when …" He looked away, shamefaced.

Fitz opened the drawer, took out the phone and dropped it into a zip lock bag, before tucking it into an inside pocket. "We would have gotten it, you know. This just makes it a whole lot easier. Thank you. Now I'm going to need your password or words, the name or names you used in your, uh, communications, and anything else you can think of that will help us to create a profile for this guy."

The man looked totally defeated. Fitz knew he was supposed to keep his personal feelings out of his work, but he wasn't always successful. Who wouldn't feel sorry for this poor bugger—oops, wrong word. The man in the bed in front of him was physically, emotionally and spiritually shattered, all because he gave in to an urge that some would call revolting, some would say was unnatural, and his own holy mother Catholic Church would describe as a mortal sin. A sin of such major proportions that it required a true confession and honest repentance plus endless strings of "Hail Marys" to get beyond it.

But if it was God who gave us humans those urges in

the first place, who was to say they were revolting? Fitz didn't have an answer for that, and it bugged the hell out of him. Logic was not something you found in his Church. That bugged him, too.

"Detective?"

Fitz snapped himself out of his mental meander and reentered the present.

"My wife doesn't want a divorce."

"It does my heart good to hear that. That makes two for today."

"So what's number one?"

"You. You're a brave man, Winslow Bishop. This is going to get worse before it gets better. But with your cooperation, now it will get better. Best case scenario, we get the bastard and put him away for good, and you will be giving us the first real chance at doing this. That damn sure spells bravery in my book."

The man in the bed turned his head to the side but not before a tear broke loose and made its way over his cheekbone and dropped down onto the pillow.

44

"*Hey you, since you asked, I'll tell you. I do my best work after dark, if you get my drift. The darker the better. But it's too damn cold for anything alfresco for this beach bum right now. Let's start with a drink somewhere and then we can let nature take its course and make it happen. Tell me where to pick you up. Weekends are the best for me, but as they say around here, any port-hole in a storm, right?*"

LOOKING GOOD! The man was sitting alone at his computer, and the dog was still barking in the next unit, but things were definitely looking up.

He swung his hands high over his head in a silent victory salute. He knew that so many of the closeted ones chickened out at the last minute. If, and it was a big if, this one took the bait and swallowed it, he'd be back on schedule and wouldn't even need that set of scrubs he'd found at Walmart. With a little luck he could dispatch this one in a week or two before getting back onto the schedule for his original number three.

He didn't like rushing things. He was a man of precision and deliberation. But the failure had thrown everything off, and he knew there was no way to relieve the mounting tension creeping into his very bones without getting number two out of the way first.

Ordinarily the thrill of the chase, the slow build up, the dirty language foreplay, was part of the game, part of the thrill. He loved building that tension, putting it all together piece by piece like an exquisite sculpture, but he'd never failed before. The final dispatching of the victim is what broke that exquisite, titillating and deliciously aching awful tension for him, not the sex. That was only foreplay. It was the surprise kill that did it for him. After this one he'd be back on his game and back on schedule, and he'd be one hell of a lot less agitated. He'd be able to take his time on the next one.

After that, if it was humanly possible, he'd give himself a little down time at the B&B before starting his next trilogy. He needed a little break. No, he needed a big break this time.

45

At two minutes after two in the afternoon, Kevin Daly rang the front doorbell at what would be his place of residence for the upcoming three months. He had a computer case slung over one shoulder, a bouquet of flowers under his arm and was holding onto the handle of a black four-wheeled "weekender."

Viridienne opened the door and smiled. "Welcome to La Vie en Rose, Kevin. I don't see your car. Have you already parked in the back?"

"I have indeed, Viridienne, and thank you for allowing me that. Here," he let go of the suitcase and held out the flowers. "These are for you and your sister."

Viridienne accepted the flowers and stood aside so that Kevin could come in. "I suspect you know the way to your room. Just so you know, I went in there the other day and opened the window and gave it a good airing and dusting and a swipe with the broom so it would be nice and fresh when you arrived."

Something flashed across the man's face, but it was so

quick, it could have been nothing more than a twitch. "That's very kind of you, Viridienne, but I will ask that from now on, you not go onto my room unannounced. You didn't touch anything, did you?" In an uncomfortable moment, his engaging smile was gone, and he looked positively stricken.

"Oh, good heavens no, not a thing. But we always change the linens for the guests and …"

He held up his hand and recovered his smile. "Of course, you do, and it's more than kind. But since you are giving me such a discounted rate, I'll be happy take care of anything like that myself. If you'll just leave the clean things on the little table outside the door, I'll take them in, and then leave you the things that need to be laundered. I'll leave the rent money there as well. I'll put it in an envelope with your name on it."

"But …"

He shook his head. "I must insist, dear lady. Now, why don't you go and put those flowers into some water, and I'll get myself settled in. Oh, yes, and there's one other thing I should mention. You kindly gave me a back door key, and if it's all the same to you, I'll probably be using that door rather than the front door so I won't disrupt you all by my comings and goings. I told you, I keep odd hours."

He shrugged and added an apologetic smile as if to underscore his determination to be as little bother as possible. "It's the blessing and the curse of the self-employed consultant. We need to be available whenever a client calls in. Still," another shrug, "it pays the rent." He smiled, held up his key, turned away and walked down the narrow hallway toward his room.

Viridienne carried the flowers into the kitchen and set about looking for a suitable vase. She was trying to understand why she was feeling so unsettled and trying harder to explain it away by telling herself she just wasn't used to having a long-term resident. Even if he was off by himself at the back of the house. Even if, as he said, she'd likely never hear him go out or come in. Why did that somehow make her sense of unease even worse?

The flowers, pink and red carnations this time, were cheery enough. She cut the stems, dropped them into a bowl of water, and then flower by flower set them into an old white porcelain teapot she often used for floral arrangements. When she finished, she topped up the water and carried them into the sitting room, set them on the coffee table and stepped back to admire the effect. Not too big, not over the top or extravagant, just a nice touch, a gracious touch. So what was her problem?

"What do you think, cat?" She turned toward the couch, where DT usually camped out during the day, but the cat was nowhere to be seen. "DT? Where are you, boy? DT?"

At the repeated sound of his name, the one-eyed orange feline slithered out of the corner of the bookcase and trotted across the room to her side. Viridienne reached down and gave him a chin scratch and wondered if he was feeling poorly. Ordinarily, he did not wedge himself into small out of sight places unless he was not feeling well. She picked him up, no small accomplishment considering his size, and looked him in his one eye. "You all right, kiddo?"

DT was a cat to be reckoned with, not trifled with. He had any number of discernible facial expressions, and this one was worried and uneasy. His single eye was wide, his two ears slightly back, and his body tense. She felt his ears. They were cool to the touch. No fever.

"Something you ate? Something that you killed first and

then ate that didn't go down too well? She knew it couldn't be tinsel off the tree, because she hadn't used any. Then she wondered whether he'd tried to eat a few fallen pine needles, or ingested a bit of ribbon?

"Okay, big boy, we'll just keep an eye on you for the next twenty-four hours, and if need be, we'll go and see Doctor Mary."

The name of the vet was enough to send the animal galloping out of the room and off toward the kitchen. That cat's no fool, thought Viridienne. I wonder if there's something he's not telling me.

itz powered up the clandestine-work-only tablet he kept for operations like this. He'd registered it in a false name and opened an account on a free email service that was riddled with spam and questionable political advertisements. It was no doubt much in the same way that the man he was targeting had done: No traceable record, no electronic trail of crumbs. He tapped "Men looking for men" into the search engine.

After reading the directions for submission and then reading several of the ads to use as a guideline, he began to write.

"Hi out there, I'm new to the South Shore and I'm looking for someone to show me the sights. I'm not into long-term commitments, so if that's what you're after, I'm not your man. A quick quiet rendezvous in an out-of-the-way place is the way I do things. First names only, I'll even buy the drinks. Redd-Baronn."

It was his first ever personal ad, and when he re-read it, after one final hesitation, he hit Send. Then, before he lost his rhythm and his stomach, he wrote a second ad using a different name.

"Do you like to play school? Are you a naughty schoolboy? Would you like to be one? I'm into stern headmaster play-acting and bad-boy spanking. Under the right circumstances I can be a very bad boy, or you can be the bad boy and I can discipline you. Turn-about is fair play, right? Why don't you sign up for one of my night courses? HEAD-MASTERTOM"

Fitz was feeling an uncomfortable fascination in doing this. The writer and the closeted actor in him relished the intellectual challenge. The gentleman, the scholar, the old school Catholic and the ethicist in him wanted to throw up.

He was still waiting on forensic information from the experts before he could undertake anything official on this investigation, but this wasn't investigation. This was research. Information gathering. He was testing very murky waters, and all of it strictly off the record. The question that hung in the air over his head and unsettled his stomach was, would this be an empty shot in the dark, or would it be the beginning of a grim reaping? Fitz had learned a long time ago that sometimes the best way to fight fire was with fire. But it was dangerous and tricky business, because fires can backfire. He turned his attention to his tablet and the work at hand, but in reality, all he could do now, was wait.

It didn't take any kind of expert to see how these ads were written and what kind of person responded. Fitz was not good at waiting and was very good at conducting his own investigations, using his own, sometimes unorthodox, methods in the process. This, however, was a first. He'd never considered looking for companionship on line. Not ever.

His slowly developing relationship with the lanky, slightly obsessive artist, who was more recently the owner-manager of a Victorian B&B that overlooked the center of town and the harbor beyond, was more than enough for this late-blooming Irishman. That image and all the delightful promise that it carried with it should be enough to calm his racing mind, even for a minute or two. But it wasn't.

He blinked away the pleasant thought and returned to the muck and misery on the table in front of him. He was going through conversations on Bishop's single use private phone himself before handing it over to forensics.

Through the wondrous mysteries of technology, he was able to print out several of the conversations onto sheets of paper. These he spread out on the desk in front of him, examining the visual shapes and spaces in the communications and looking for repeated patterns. After doing this, he would go back online and look up some of the seamier matching sites to see if he could find any immediate comparisons to what he had in front of him. No question about it, there was plenty for him to look through, but on that first go-through he found nothing that was even remotely close.

Fitz found the advertisements to be profoundly depressing and, in more than a few instances, simply revolting. If he weren't so bothered by what he was delving into, he might have enjoyed the challenge of writing a truly enticing letter, purely as an academic exercise. He did, after all, have a degree in literature. But as a graduate student in Irish literature and poetry at Trinity College in Dublin, this was something he could never have imagined—writing phony letters of illicit enticement to lure, entrap and hopefully catch a sadistic killer. How the mighty have fallen.

Still he was struggling. Online dating was commonplace now. Perfectly legal. In fact, it was big business. The obvious question for him was why wasn't the law doing more about this kind of thing, the online stalking, grooming, exploitation, buying and selling of human bodies and souls? Then he answered his own question: If you build it, they will come. If you sell it, they will buy. If you want it, you can find it, all for a price.

There it was, right in front of him. There would always be a ready shadow-market for what these people were buying, selling and/or offering for free. The grim reality was it had been there since time began. Would his efforts amount to anything other than a ripple on this current sea of shit? Maybe yes, maybe no, but it would make a difference to Winn Bishop and possibly bring him one step closer to finding the man that attacked him. So yes, it was worth it. But what then? Winn Bishop was one man, one sad and desperate man. Could he, Detective Fitzpatrick, stem the larger stinking tide? Fitz was an optimist, but he wasn't a fool. He was, however, a man of faith with a conscience built on experience and a deep commitment to doing the right thing when he could. This case would test everything he believed in.

His private tablet bleeped, alerting him to an incoming message. It would appear that someone calling himself DICK van DIKE, had replied to Redd-Baronn.

Fitz didn't know whether to feel good or bad about getting such a quick response. He did know it saddened him beyond all measure that such connections were so easily made. In the end he decided both feelings were valid. A hollow victory, to be sure, and a victory with more and worse to come.

He toyed with the idea of responding at once but realized he wasn't ready to take this any further. This was a test run. This was the first casting out of the bait, and it was still floating around out there. He needed to wait and see who or what else would strike at the hook. And when. On the other hand, if he'd actually come upon the triple serial killer, the mysterious man who killed gay men in threes, he didn't have much time.

He was convinced that setting up a sting and trying to trap the guy was his best bet. But Fitz wasn't a betting man, and even to him, this would be a very long shot. He'd go see Winn Bishop again, and after that, once the forensics were back, he'd kick it all into high gear.

Then he hit Reply.

47

Viridienne was in the sitting room, contemplating undecorating the tree. Should she start now or keep it up until New Year's Day when so many families ritually took down the tree? She liked having it there, even if it was drying out and dropping needles everywhere. She loved the piney smell.

From where she was sitting, she could hear the very faintest sounds of a TV coming from the room at the end of the hall. It was a pleasant sound. A human sound, not at all disturbing or intrusive. She smiled. It meant he was in. It was strange having a guest and not making him breakfast, but she had to admit, it was a heck of a lot easier. It meant she was on nobody's schedule but her own, and she was still making money. Maybe the long-term rental thing won't be so bad after all, she thought. But it's not bad, you silly woman, it's just different, that's all. Get over it, will you?

"I'll give you until the New Year," she said to the tree, "but only if you promise not to drop any more needles."

"Who in the world are you talking to? DT's in the kitchen."

"The Christmas tree, of course."

"Of course. Silly me." Em dropped down onto the far end of the sofa and propped her feet up on the coffee table.

Viridienne explained that she had considered taking it down but decided in the end to wait until January first.

"And does the tree have anything to say about it?"

Viridienne threw a pillow at her sister and said, "It told me to stop needling it, and that it's just pining to stay up until then."

Emily threw the pillow back and pointed in the direction of the music.

"I take it he's in, then. I was upstairs. Never heard a thing."

Viridienne nodded. "It's weird not having to check on him like a regular guest. I guess that's the difference between a guest and a renter."

"What do you mean?"

"A guest is someone we look after and check in with and feed breakfast to. A renter books his room, pays his rent, and we shut the door and leave him alone. A guest is a guest in our home. A paying guest, but a guest nonetheless. They come, they go, and we cater to them, and we pamper them. For the time that Kevin is renting that room from us, it's his room, his home really." She held up both hands. "It's all hands *off* deck for us while he's here."

She paused and looked at her sister. "You know me. I need to work out the order of things and how they fit together. I need definitions, and I think I just sorted myself out on this one. He's a renter. In three months, he'll move out." She made the wiping-hands-I'm-through-with-it-gesture. "Done and dusted."

"But how will we know if he's in or out?"

"Technically, it's none of our business, but use your head, girl. There will be a light under the door, we will hear the TV or a radio, and the easiest and most obvious of all?"

"What's that?"

"If his car is here, he's here. If it's not, he's not."

"Unless he decides to go for a walk."

"You've got a point, but I don't expect he'll be doing too much of that in this cold. Maybe when it gets warmer. But seriously, Em, the man is renting a room. He can come and go as he wishes, and he can do it through his own entrance. Other than keeping the heat up and electricity on and the hot and cold water running, he's none of our concern really."

"I know, but …"

"Don't worry. By the time we've completely adjusted, he'll be gone. Then we can decide whether or not to do it again. End of topic." Viridienne paused and shifted gears. "Now then, what about you? Anything new from your navy man?"

Em grinned and flashed a thumb's up at her sister.

"Shall I take that as a yes?"

"He says he's hoping to be here for Valentine's day."

"Well, that's exciting. Any more details?"

"Not yet. I guess there's a lot of stuff has to be check and okayed. Military paperwork, he says. It's vacation week at school for me, and we're not terribly busy here, and my part-time job is flexible, so…" She stopped and took a deep breath.

'What is it Em?"

She looked away and chewed on her lip for a moment. "I don't really know. I mean it was all fun and exciting when he was off and away. Now that he's actually coming, and I'm going to meet him, all of a sudden I feel all butter-fly-ish inside." She put her hand on her stomach.

"Sounds pretty normal to me, Em. What will be, will be. Just take it one day at a time."

Viridienne smiled and tried to look as though she really meant it. Later, in the privacy of her own room, she would go back online and see what else she could find on You-Me-We.

At the end of the hallway, double-locked safely in his room, Kevin Daly, his nom-du-mois, was unpacking and settling in. With the TV droning on, making a meaningless white noise in the background, he set about ordering his space. First came the hanging clothes, the dark ones first and after that the light ones, shirts, slacks, suits in order and arranged according to color, all freshly cleaned and pressed and evenly spaced. Underwear, socks and handkerchiefs, rolled and tucked into the top drawer. Casual shirts and pants under that, and lower still a portable radio, his charging devices and a small steel combination lock box.

Under the bed he put the steel suitcase that he'd wheeled in with him that afternoon. This was the one that contained his working tools: surgical gloves, sterile wipes, latex facial enhancements, make up, an assortment of wigs and toupees, and a small supply of his date rape drug of choice. Finally, there was an almost full box of the plastic tie strips that many police departments use as handcuffs, and he used to complete the assault. The trick was to have it out and at the ready before the mark ever saw it coming. This last time he'd missed a beat, and the whole thing had gone south. But he was back on track now, and that would never happen again. As insurance, he would spend some time practicing. Practice makes perfect, and perfect is good.

He couldn't help but chuckle at the irony of it all. Here

he was in an upscale B&B not a mile from where he'd last struck, living with two dear sweet ladies and a cat with only one eye that ran the other way when he came in. Two ladies who could not be safer from his phishing inquiries if they had an armed guard on site. Why, he might even offer to take out the trash now and then just to demonstrate how very sincere and helpful a tenant he was. Local ladies were never part of his plan. His targets were the distant, stupid, needy ones who were out there begging to be caught.

And the googly-eyed, love-struck cop. The whole thing was just too funny for words. Funny and perfect. But don't ever get so comfortable and sure of yourself that you drop your guard again, you dumb bastard, he told himself. Play the game, but make sure you play by the rules.

"I'M GOING out for a little while, Vid. You need anything?" Emily stood in the doorway to the sitting room.

"Nope, I'm good for now, and we're both good for supper. Leftovers on toast with gravy. I'm thinking about New Year's Day, though, maybe having a special tea and inviting over a few friends, maybe even asking our tenant to join us if he's willing to come out of his nest. I need to think about that a little longer, and when I do decide, I'll do the shopping myself."

"Um, you don't have much time."

"I'm not planning much. We'll see."

"Are you and Fitz going to be doing anything special on New Year's Eve?"

Viridienne laughed and shook her head. "Would you believe that thought never occurred to me? Maybe I should ask. I don't think of us as an item yet. He's a special friend, and he's working on a big case right now. So who knows? I never made a big thing of New Year's Eve in the past, and I don't much care to now. Screaming and yelling and getting drunk and staying up half the night and feeling like dried vomit on the next day never was my idea of a good time. Maybe you and I, or we three, might just play Scrabble by the fire. We can open a bottle of champagne around nine, so I can be in bed by ten."

It was Emily's turn to chuckle. "Meet my sister, always the life of the party. She sure knows how to have a good time."

"Are you going out, or are you just going to stand there disrespecting your elder?"

"I'm going out. Now. If you change your mind and decide you do want something, call me."

48

With only two days to go until the long New Year weekend, Fitz was under the gun, metaphorically speaking. He wanted to move forward on this case ASAP, but because of the reduced staff, he was not able to move at the speed he would have preferred. He did, by now, have preliminary reports from forensics. The blood on the trousers and the gloves matched that of Winslow Bishop, and there was clearly identifiable DNA from that of a second person, the would-be murderer, Individual B. That was the good news. The bad news was that there was nothing anywhere in any info-bank that had a registered match to the DNA of the assailant. Still, he was further ahead than anyone else involved in these mysterious and troubling cases, and it was all thanks to a smelly, hungry homeless man who saw something and then said something.

He called Alison at home and explained that he really needed a sounding board and asked if she might be willing to come into the office.

"Sure, Fitz, give me an hour." He didn't even have to bribe her with coffee or lunch, but being the man he was, he would provide it anyway.

When she arrived the coffee was waiting for her, and so was Fitz, with his tablet powered up, his new Redd-Baronn profile and now seventeen responses and counting on full display.

"Holy shit," said Alison. She was not a woman given to idle chatter. "When did you post that?"

"This morning."

She shook her head in amazement as much as disbelief. "I guess they really are all out there. So now what?"

"Well, it is my case." Then he corrected himself, "Our case, when you get back."

She waved him off. "Good God man, please don't fuss about the details. I'm hardly possessive. This one's all yours, and I'm the back-up. Next time we switch sides. So what's your plan?"

"If the guy sticks to his pattern, he's going to go after number three before long. He might even have the poor unsuspecting bastard in the cross hairs already."

"But it won't really be number three. Number two was a misfire. Do you think he'll try and keep it at the magic three and go after another one?"

"The pattern and frequency of the others says yes, and my gut says yes. Putting the two together tells me we need to kick this into high gear."

Alison cocked her head. "You know, I could come up with a different persona and work from home, if you want. You know, spread a bigger net? I could cc you and you could cc me on everything we get, then compare notes. Two heads are always better than one, especially when one of them is mine."

Fitz gut-punched himself and said, "Ugh! You really know how to take a man down, don't you?"

She smirked. "Years of practice sparring with two older brothers."

"Okay, then, enough of this wild hilarity. Who are you going to be?"

"Hmmm, let me think. If you're Red-Baronn, how about me being, Grey Foxx? You know, as in Grey, my last name, and Foxx?"

"Works for me. Let's see if it works for you. Between the two of us, if the guy is out there looking, we stand a good chance of at least getting a hit."

"But how will we know it, if or when we do?"

Fitz went silent for a moment and then said, "I guess we start with the facts as we have them, and then we go on spit and adrenalin. The detective's gut, the third eye. Who the hell knows? I just know I can't sit around and wait for this SOB to strike again." He pointed to the calendar on the wall.

"My gut tells me he's still in the area, that he has one mark in the queue and he's out looking for fresh meat. Let's go have something to eat, then you go home and turn yourself into a shadow of your former self and get on to it. I'll go see Winn Bishop and go over it all again with him. Poor guy. He is so ashamed by all of this."

"No surprise," said Alison. "Why does it have to be this way?"

"It's a bigger question than I have an answer for. Something to do with the narrow ways we cast ourselves and others. What's right and what's wrong, as opposed to what's the nature of human nature, good and evil, all that stuff. But right now we don't have the luxury of philosophizing on the subject. We need to get out there and see if we can find ourselves a serial killer."

"What do I do for a picture?"

"Wait until they ask for one, and then Photoshop something. I haven't put one up yet either, but that's what I'm going to do."

"Okay. You go on then. I'm going to stay and work here. I don't want to do this at home."

Alison went downstairs to the supply desk and requested a dark tablet of her own. Tucking it into her purse, she returned to their shared office on the second floor and settled down to business.

"Hi there, I'm new to all of this, and I'm not really out and I need someone to talk to. Not ready for a real date yet either, so maybe a cup of coffee somewhere? I could really use a friend. Are you the guy? I'm in my early thirties, I'm an investment banker by day, when I'm not in my business suit and tie, I play bass in a jazz trio. You can contact me @ Grey Foxx on the site directory."

When she finished, she went home and had a very long, very hot shower, and still she felt unclean.

49

With everything unpacked, sorted and arranged in his customary meticulous order, Kevin sat down in the easy chair to contemplate his next move. By now it was almost supper time, and he was more than ready for something to eat, but his stomach was in knots. He couldn't stop obsessing about how much the guy he attacked would be able to tell the police. By now the media had dropped it, but that didn't mean the police had. Not by a long shot. Kevin was well aware of that, and to coin a phrase, it was eating his lunch.

He'd gotten rid of the trousers and the gloves with the blood on them, but at the time of the attack, the victim had clawed at him and broken the skin. His own DNA was out there now. All those years of staying out of the data banks were history. From this day forward there would be no second chance. He could never let down his guard or leave a trace of himself anywhere ever again. As much of a challenge as this was going to be, he would just have to add it to the growing list of the many things he could, could not, and was required to do in order to get through the day.

He would wear gloves everywhere. Wash or burn anything he inadvertently touched or that touched him. Wash his own bedsheets. He already did his own laundry; he'd just add the sheets and towels to the list. He'd explain to Viridienne that he'd developed a skin condition which required the gloves and a special detergent, and because of that he always carried his own linens with him.

With this new pattern taking shape in his mind, Kevin began to relax. Order was what he needed above all else, order and predictability that he alone was responsible for constructing. As long as he had a structure, a carapace of safety around him at all times, he could function. With that back in place, he could set about finding himself some food. He considered his options.

He could call for a takeout. He could eat some of the granola bars he kept for emergency rations when he knew he was going to miss a meal, or he could walk down the hill and find himself a pizza place or a sandwich shop where he'd be just another nameless face at the counter.

His belly voted for option three, not to mention that the walk would do him no end of good. He needed some fresh air in his lungs after all of this, and while he was out he would pick up those few food basics he liked to keep on hand.

His room was equipped with an electric teakettle, cups, saucers and two drinking glasses. In one of the unmarked boxes he'd moved in earlier was a very small microwave and a sub-mini-portable fridge. Miracles of technology, really, and it amazed him when he learned such things existed. They made his independence, his transience and near anonymous self-sufficiency almost perfect. Almost.

The cellular/chemical anonymity was gone now, but he had the facial image thing under control, and that was because it kept changing courtesy of makeup, cheek packing and enhancements, or like right now, partial obfuscation.

He pulled a nondescript knitted hat low on his forehead, making sure to cover his eyebrows, wound a scarf up over his mouth and added a pair of tinted glasses. His winter jacket, a monster of a down thing from an upscale sporting goods store, was designed to cover and visually neutralize anyone inside it. He looked like anyone else would look in the wintertime on the streets of Plymouth, an anonymous man going out after dark for a quick bite to eat. If he wanted a drink, he would have it when he got home. The last thing he wanted to do was set foot in a bar or a restaurant he might want to use as a future rendezvous point and later have someone think of him as vaguely familiar.

Tonight, he would leave the light on and radio playing in his absence. He would go out and return using the back door. With his car it its allotted parking space and sounds of a human presence coming from his room, he could get some practice in slipping in and out whenever he wanted to. Yes, things were definitely coming back into focus.

Kevin smiled. Talk about falling into a shit-pile and coming up with a rose. He really thought he was well and truly finished the other night, but as fate would have it, it would appear to be exactly the opposite. Location, location, location. It really was everything.

All of this notwithstanding, the unbearable push-pull inside him was mounting. It was like a time-bomb, a detonated grenade inside his chest and in his brain, ticking down to explosion. The compulsive urges were getting stronger. He'd never gotten to the place of actual explosion. He'd always managed to make a hit and diffuse that sweet-awful agony before he imploded. But this time he'd missed, and the tension was still building, making his head pound and his ears ring with the loathsome longing of it all. He'd scheduled the original number three for Valentine's Day and saw no point in changing that. So maybe he should aim for January 6th, for his new number two. By the looks of it, he had a good one lined up. It was the day some people referred to as Little Christmas, the day when the three kings were said to have come to the stable with their gifts for the holy child. That works, he thought. Holidays, big ones or local ones, gave him a ready theme to work with. A ready framework added to his credulity. And by the looks of it, he had at least two in the pipeline, a guy calling himself Redd-Baronn and another one who couldn't spell, but because of that might be easier to roll. The Baronn guy sounded a little slick. On the other hand, the minute he saw the word "discreet" in a profile, it screamed anonymity to him and a man who would go to any lengths to stay that way.

Now all he had to do was decide on the man who would be the next number two in the sequence. When he got back after his supper, he'd sit down with a glass of something relaxing beside him, look over his prospects one more time and make his decision. Now that he had a plan, he could go find himself something to eat and be able to digest it.

He eased the door to his room open and listened for sounds in the house. Low voices in the kitchen. Perfect. If someone did appear, he'd just tell them the truth. He was going out for a bite to eat, and he'd be sure they saw him get into the car and drive it away. If he did get out unseen, but then someone saw him coming back or he bumped into one of them on the street, he'd say exactly the same thing:

he was out for a bite to eat and a breath of fresh air and to stretch his legs, then add, "My, isn't it cold out this evening?" before hurrying on.

He pulled the back door shut behind him without making a sound that any human could hear. But cats are a different story. DT's ears went up and then back, and he padded softly and purposefully out of the kitchen.

"What do you suppose caught his attention? I didn't hear anything, did you?" Inside the kitchen the sisters were contemplating what they would have for supper over cups of fresh coffee.

Emily shook her head. "Animals can hear and sense things that we can't, no surprise to you. We had a cat back when I was still in the Society that knew when someone was going to die. He'd go into the room, hop up onto the bed and stay there, purring, until the person crossed over. It was uncanny, but it was nice. Comforting, I guess."

Viridienne pushed back her chair and stood up. "Well, I'll go have a look-see anyway, just because cats hear things we can't. We're still new at having a long-term renter here, and I want to make sure he didn't leave the water running in the bathroom or there's a mouse on the loose back there."

In less than a minute she was back. "All good. He's in. The light and radio are on in his room, the car's in the drive, and DT is sitting guard outside the door. We both know that silly cat can't stand a closed door. Whatever side he is on, he wants to be on the other one."

Emily rolled her eyes. "Cats! They are what they are, but I have to admit you got yourself a prizewinner when you got him."

Viridienne's eyes misted over. "Poor little bugger. He had one hour left when I came into the shelter that day.

Because of the one eye, they said he was unadoptable. It was love at first bite. Did I tell you he bit me when I first picked him up? Not hard, just a love nibble. He still does it sometimes, chews on a finger or my thumb when he's really happy."

But outside of Kevin's room at the back of the house, DT was not happy, nor was he chasing a mouse. In the uncanny way that animals have of knowing more than they can say with words, he sounded the alarm in the only was he could. He got up from his crouch, turned himself butt-to-the door, lifted his tail and fired off a long, warm, well-aimed stream of pee.

50

It was cold and getting dark when Fitz left his office and headed for his car. What he really wanted to do was to go straight home, or alternatively give Viridienne a call and see if he could come over for a mug of tea before checking in on his mother. In the end he decided against both options. Duty was calling. A surprise visit to Winn Bishop at the end of the day, when the man would be tired and less on guard, could be quite productive in terms of information gathering. Sad, though, when he considered that he, Homicide Detective Fitz was probably the last man on the face of this earth that the poor guy wanted to see.

"Hi, Winn.: He paused and gave him a double thumbs up. "I say you *are* looking better. They gonna let you out soon?"

Bishop nodded. "Probably tomorrow."

"I've been looking at your phone, and I've got a few questions." Fitz did a double take. "Jaysus, man, you're getting out tomorrow? You haven't told anyone where you'll be going yet, have you?"

"Haven't decided where it'll be yet, so no. Why?"

"Winn, there's a guy out there who tried to kill you. I don't want to scare you, but I do need to warn you. It's entirely possible he might try and come back and finish what he started. That's why we had someone here in the hospital keeping an eye on you. We can keep that detail on you, if you'd like."

"Oh, God no. The last goddamn thing I want is to draw any more attention to myself. No!"

"I can't make you do it if you don't want to, but I can ask that you tell no one other than me and your wife where you are. And wherever it is, keep the doors and windows locked. Keep my personal number on speed dial, and until we get him, don't ever go out alone. I promise you this, Winn. We will get him. He's the lowest kind of scumbag there is. He tricks good men into believing his trash talk, preys on their supposed…" Fitz made air quotes with his fingers. "…weakness and the desperate need for secrecy, and he knows just the right words to stoke the fire."

Winn covered his face with his hands as Fitz continued.

"It's not weakness, and it's not a disease, man, it's human. Some people play for one side, some people play for the other, and some people switch-hit. What you are isn't shameful, but how you dealt with it almost killed you. There has to be a better way for all of you."

"But my wife, my kids …"

"I'm not getting into the marriage vows here, that's different, and it's for you two to work through. You aren't the first, and you won't be the last man or woman on earth who's ever strayed. The only thing I wish I could take away is the shame. I know you've heard it before, but Rome wasn't built in a day, and changing people's attitudes about things of this nature is going to take longer than that. The good news is, you're not dead. You could have been. That means we still have time."

Winn took his hands away from his face and looked up at the

man standing next to his bed and pointed to the chair. "Time for what? You said something about more questions?"

"I did. I've been going over the thread of emails you had with that guy on your phone, and I think I might be detecting the beginnings of a pattern. That's what I want to ask you about. Things like what time of day did he typically do his writing to you? Did he respond quickly or wait a couple of hours or even a day or two before answering?"

"Isn't that all on the phone? Can't you get it off of there? Don't get me wrong, I know you're trying to help me, but it feels like you're rubbing my nose in it. Saying it all out loud over and over again makes me just want to go off somewhere and blow my brains out. That would take care of it all, wouldn't it?"

Fitz snapped to attention. "Winn, are you likely to try and take your own life? Tell me the truth."

Bishop held up one hand and looked off to the side. "Crap, no. I'm too chicken. I will tell you there have been times since this whole thing happened and before, for that matter, when I thought a massive coronary wouldn't be the worst thing in the world. It would've solved all my problems for me, and I wouldn't have had to go buy a gun. What I really want is for everything to go away, just go away, but since it's not going to, I guess the only way out of all this is forward."

"Do you mind if I use the tape recorder again?"

"Look, just sit down and get it the fuck over with, will you?"

51

Kevin Daly, wrapped and swathed and bespectacled beyond recognition, clumped along the main street of Plymouth, window shopping for his supper. When he was out on the streets, he even altered the way he walked. A person's stride is almost as identifiable as a fingerprint or a signature, and Kevin had several different walks to choose from. Tonight, it was a side-to-side, heavy-footed clumping with a definite left-right, swing-sway rhythm.

Sometimes he carried a backpack slung over one shoulder, other times, a cross-body messenger bag. This evening he lumped along, looking down at the sidewalk in front of him, hands stuffed in his pockets, carrying nothing at all.

He was a student of human nature. He studied people's walks. He studied gestures, body language and rhythms of speech. In another life he would have made an excellent character actor. He was an obsessive-compulsive chameleon of a man who was a serial killer of closeted gay men and who supported himself by phishing for gullible, love-starved women who were only too happy to send him all the money he asked for. But at the moment, he was nothing more than a hungry man in search of something to eat.

Attracted by the smells of garlic, hot cheese and tomato sauce, and the fact that there was a fair number of people crowded around the counter he could blend into and never be noticed, he turned into a restaurant. The noise of shouted orders and clattering dishes, the good-natured joking and jostling, were perfect cover. He looked up at the menu board and decided that a large steak and cheese, broiled open faced with a double shot of hot peppers on the side, would fill the bill.

Ten minutes later, with the sandwich tucked inside his jacket, staying hot and serving as a chest warmer, Daly was back on the sidewalk, stumping up the hill toward his temporary home. He'd stuffed a bag of chips in one pocket and a handful of napkins and a bottle of Diet Coke in the other. As he walked along, he made a note-to-self to save a scrap of steak and a bit of cheese for his landlady's one-eyed cat; he'd already forgotten its name. It never hurts to have friends in high places or to curry favor and admiration from those beneath you. With every step the smell of the sandwich grew stronger, and the rumbles from his stomach grew more insistent. He tried to pick up his speed, but the frigid air fought back. It was seriously cold out there.

Chilled and winded from the walk up the hill in the icy air, he was happy to be back in the warm. He checked to see that his car and everything in his room was exactly as he left it. It was. He wanted to check the news on the television, but that could come later. Business before pleasure always, but in this case he had the opportunity to kill two birds with one stone. He could eat supper and check the phishing lines at the same time.

He unwrapped his supper and spread it out beside the computer. There were a couple of responses to his most recent posting that looked promising and, to his grim satisfaction, several new listings that appeared to be worth investigating. He was beginning to relax. By the number and quality of the responses on the screen in front of him, it was a near certainty he would keep his promise to himself and stay on schedule.

Daly bit into his still hot sandwich and for a brief moment gave himself over to the total sensuality of the experience. The warmth of the fresh bread in his hands and in his mouth, the contrast of the runny cheese and the crisp baguette, the garlicy-steaky smell, even the hastily wiped off grease that ran down his chin was all part of the magic of comfort food—that and having a plan. Kevin liked it when things fell into place.

FITZ WAS on his way home that afternoon when his cell phone bleeped and Alison's name flashed on the dash-screen.

"Can you believe I've already got six hits? What do I do now?"

"You package them up, do absolutely nothing and come into the office tomorrow morning. Is that possible? I think it would be better for us to work side by side on this rather than online."

"Fitz?"

"Yeah?"

"This is freakin' nasty. I am totally weirded out."

"It's all that and then some, but you can't let it get to you. Having said that, I'll be the first to add, that's easier said than done. Buckle up, partner, I think we're going to be in for a rough patch on this one. Hang in there. Take notes, and we'll dig into it tomorrow."

52

W hen Daly rolled out of bed the following morning, he smelled something. It was not the remnants of his sandwich wafting up from the cast-off wrappings in the wastebasket, nor was it any of the multi-fragrances arranged carefully in his toiletries kit. He sat on the edge of the bed and sniffed at the air around him. It has been said that smells are strongly evocative of personal memories, and this was not a good memory. This was redolent of the run-down government-owned housing projects where he grew up, of squalid back alleys and stray dogs and cats scavenging through already picked over garbage, desperate for something to eat. Like a bloodhound, he followed his nose, sniffing, to the door of his room and to a dark spot just inside it. Cat piss. Once experienced, it was never forgotten. There could be only one perpetrator on site, and that would be DT.

He pulled on the clothes he'd left lying over a near-by chair, unlocked the door of his room and listened. As on the night before, he could hear voices in the kitchen. He walked with a heavier tread than he usually did so the sisters would hear him coming and not be startled. Then to be absolutely sure, he cleared his throat and tapped on the door frame.

"Well, look what the cat dragged in," said Viridienne with a wave to join them at the table. "Want some coffee? We just made it."

He shook his head. "No, thanks, ladies. I'll make some later in my room, I'm still waking up. Um, I came to report a little problem. I think the cat might have had an accident outside my door."

"What! He never does that. You're sure it's cat?"

"Once smelled, never forgotten. I'm sure it's an accident. He probably couldn't get out in time."

Viridienne looked genuinely horrified and immediately stood up. "I am so sorry, some welcome for the new guest. I'll clean it up right now."

He held up his hand. "No, that's alright, I'd rather do it myself. If you have some white vinegar and water and a sponge, I'll be all set. I've had cats, and I know all the tricks."

"Kevin, that's really kind of you, but it's above and beyond the line of duty. It's my job to keep your place of residence not only clean but homey and welcoming. I wonder whatever got into him."

"Whatever it was, it's easily mended, and I'll take care of it, if you don't mind. I really would prefer to. Call it quirky if you want, but I'm very particular about how I clean things."

Viridienne caught the subliminal warning in his voice and backed off.

"Of course, but …"

Daly smiled. "No buts about it. I've had cats, and cats have accidents. It wouldn't be the first time I've mopped up a puddle."

"Well, I damn sure hope it's the last," said Emily. "We'll have to have a little chat with that boy about being a better host."

Kevin held up his hand and chuckled. "Look at it this way, it could have been worse!"

Now Viridienne was laughing. "Let's not go there. I'll get you some vinegar and water. I keep it already mixed to wipe down the counters here in the kitchen."

When Daly, armed with the cleaning supplies, left the kitchen to go back to his room, Viridienne and Emily took up where they left off.

"So, Em, Let's get back to this Joe Franklin, when and where you are finally going to meet up with him."

"He told me he was able to get leave in the middle of February right around Valentine's day. Is that good omen, or is that a good omen?" Her blue eyes were dancing.

"Can't disagree with that," said Viridienne.

"I got an email this morning, saying he'd cleared it with his Captain, and barring an international incident, he'd have a whole three weeks off. He said he'd have to fly stand-by, so he won't actually know when he's going to get here until he's on the plane."

"That means you still don't know exactly when, or exactly if, he's coming."

"He gave me a two- to three-day window around the fourteenth. That's good enough for now. It's not like he's coming tomorrow, and we have to make up one of the guestrooms or anything. Geeze, Vid, stop digging, will you?"

Viridienne held up her hands in surrender. "Sorry, Em.

It's just that I've been in this world a whole lot longer than you have. I know I'm being too protective. It's a big sister thing, I guess. I'll be good, I promise."

"Vid?"

"I didn't tell you everything yesterday when Fitz was here because I thought I might bring the fires of hell down on myself. You see, he did ask to borrow some money. Just a little. Only enough to buy a new suit for when he comes to visit."

"What!" It came out as a half-gasp, half-shriek.

"I knew you'd go ballistic. That's why I didn't tell you at first."

"If he can't get snail-mail, do tell me, how did you manage to get it to him?" Viridienne's color was rising, and she was twisting her hands together in her lap to keep herself from pounding them on the table.

"He uses a PayPal account. I sent it, he ordered the suit, and the money's already back in my bank."

Viridienne didn't even try not to scream. *"You gave him your freaking bank account number?"*

"Jesus, Vid. Of course I didn't. We did it all through PayPal. I opened an account and sent it through that, and he repaid it the same way. It's totally secure, and the money is already back. He just needed to wait until he got paid. Will you just back off? You'll see when you meet him. He's nice. Very polite."

By sheer brute force of will, Viridienne ratcheted herself, and therefore the argument and the air temperature in the kitchen, down by several notches. The last thing she wanted to do was to close the lines of communication, especially now, and she could be in real danger of doing that very thing.

"I'll say it again, Em, I'm sorry. I really know better … but, well, sometimes my mouth doesn't get the message." She held up her right hand. "I hereby promise to keep my mind open and my mouth shut until further notice, or at least until such time as we are properly introduced."

"Accepted."

WHEN HE WAS SAFELY BACK in his room, and before he started scrubbing at the offending spot on the carpet, he needed to reassure himself once again that everything was in order. It was a new ritual, one that had manifested itself after he'd messed up on Christmas Eve.

Now whenever he left his room, even if it was just to go across the hall to the bathroom, he had to check out everything when he returned. There was no reason on earth to think that anyone had come in while he was in the kitchen, but it niggled at him, and he couldn't relax until he made sure everything was untouched and in place. Everything niggled at him since that awful night. Everything.

He'd screwed up, and people who screw up make stupid mistakes. He was deeply unsettled and had been ever since Christmas Eve. Everything felt like an impending threat. Every shadow was a monster. Every unexplained sound was his own death, tracking him down, getting closer and closer.

The only way he could manage and control these mounting terrors was to step up his vigilance and his orderly way of doing things. He would double, maybe even triple check everything he did. He would give careful thought to his words before saying anything to anyone. To all observers, it looked as if none of this was happening inside of him. He would be like a duck on a pond. He appeared to be effortlessly gliding along the surface of the water while frantically paddling underneath it to keep it all moving forward. It was exhausting and getting more so.

53

Fitz and Alison had been sitting side by side with their eyes glued to their respective tablets for well over three hours when lightning finally struck. They'd reached the point of physical and mental exhaustion, complete with red-rimmed stinging eye-fatigue, when they both realized they needed a break, and they needed food. The two were so tired and fog-brained that if they did come across something important, they were in real danger of missing it.

And then they saw it, or rather Fitz did. His plan had worked. There *was* a repetitive pattern in some of these communications, and he'd just spotted it.

They began that morning by printing out those messages that held any promise onto plain paper. Then one by one they superimposed one of the messages taken from Winslow Bishop's phone, printed on clear acetate, over the message they were investigating and compared the patterns made by the words and the phrases as they appeared on the printed page.

Before they started Fitz had explained to Alison, "Most people aren't actually conscious of writing in patterns, but we all do it. We repeat greetings or phrases, and our sentences follow a regular pattern, as does our spacing. We write the way we talk, and we don't really think about any of this until somebody points it out." There it was, indisputably laid out in front of them.

They were tired and hungry, but by God, they had a match. The man, now a bona fide suspect, had responded to the Redd-Baronn posting, saying that he was "Eager to know more and always up for meeting a kindred spirit … so let's make it happen."

"That's it," yelled Fitz, slamming his fist on the table between them and scaring the living crap out of his partner. "There it is, do you see it?" He was literally vibrating and pointing repeatedly at the paper on the table in front of him. See it? 'Let's make it happen' or some close variation thereof, preceded by three-dot ellipses. The same wording and the ellipses have been repeated in a number of Bishop's emails from the perp. It's as good as a signature. I think we may have our man, Alison. It's appeared in five of the nine postings, and here it is again. Now all we have to do is find him."

"Easier said than done, my friend."

He shook his head. "It won't be that hard to identify him with the technology we have today, but it goes without saying, he will have completely buried his on-line identity. That's a no-brainer, thanks to the same technology we're using right here and now. All you have to do is think about all those Russian trolls playing havoc with our elections. We know who they are and roughly where they are located, but actually laying hands on them is another challenge all together. That's going to be our problem, but we have a plan, and I will be the bait."

The two had totally forgotten that only a few minutes before, they had been tired and hungry. They'd picked up a scent, and they were totally wired and primed for the chase. The next step would be for Fitz to write back to his on-line creep and toss out more bait...more specific bait, when and where bait, and then line up his back-up team.

"Now I really do need a break," said Alison "and I need a reward, and I need some fresh air. Let's go down to Kiskadee and have a triple mocha Macchiato with double whipped cream and an orange-cranberry scone...or maybe two."

"My treat," said Fitz. He was already out of his chair and pulling on his coat.

Much as they didn't want to stop, the unwritten rule when taking a break was no talking about the job. The fact that they were in a public place underlined it in red, code red. But even more practical than that, the practice of pulling your brain totally out of a problem and overdosing it on sugar and caffeine, would ensure the energy and full attention needed when they went back to the office.

Fitz chomped into his buttered scone and let the pure bliss of the moment overtake him.

"Doing anything special on New Year's Eve?" Alison had ordered a side order of whipped cream and was slowly spooning the soft deliciousness straight into her mouth. Straight, no chaser!

"You know, I never gave it a thought. It never was something we made much of when I was a kid. Drinking yourself blind, Irish as I am, never held any attraction for me. I saw too much misery caused by the drink in my own family." He paused. "And without a lady friend to go out and about with, I just never could be bothered, but now that you've asked ..." He clapped his hand to his forehead. "What an eejit. Not only didn't I give it a thought; I didn't even give Viridienne a thought and ask her if she might like to go out for dinner or something. Methinks I'd better remedy that right this minute." Fitz pulled out his phone and asked to be excused.

Alison held up her index finger and winked. "You've been a bachelor for way too long, Fitzy-Fitz. It might be time for a change."

Funny you should say that, is what he thought, but "No comment" is what he said.

❧

Alas my love you do me wrong
To cast me off discourteously;
And I have loved you oh so long
Delighting in your company.

Greensleeves was my delight,
Greensleeves my heart of gold
Greensleeves was my heart of joy
And who but my lady Greensleeves.

I have been ready at your hand
To grant whatever thou would'st crave;
I have waged both life and land

Your love and goodwill for to have.

Greensleeves was my delight,
Greensleeves my heart of gold
Greensleeves was my heart of joy
And who but my lady Greensleeves.

54

"So, Redd-Baronn, as the old song says, 'What are you doing, New Years, New Year's Eve?' Might I ask you the same question? I don't do parties, but I do like meeting new people and maybe creating a few under cover fireworks of my own. Shall we try and make it happen?"

Daly leaned back in his chair and smiled. Only three days after Christmas. and this new one was coming on strong. The response was almost instantaneous.

"Bummer…hahaha, pun intended, I've got family shit I can't get out of. Why don't you give me a couple of other days and times? Your schedule seems to be more flexible than mine. It's tough being in the closet, but on the other hand, it makes it all so much more exciting when you do break out for a little while, don't you think? RSVP-ASAP, RB"

Holy shit, he thought, his pulse quickening, this could be the one. He typed a response, offering some alternate dates, laced with a few not-so-subtle innuendos. He needed to sound interested but not desperate. Nothing to raise the most innocent of questions in the man's mind. Questions lead to doubts, and doubts lead to back-outs.

Finally, they settled on January 6th and chose one of the local sports bars as a place to meet. A sports bar is crowded, noisy, dark and impersonal. No one takes notice of the comings and goings of the patrons, especially after a few beers and when so many of them are constantly stepping outside for a quick cigarette and God-knows-what-else throughout the evening. He turned off the computer, stood up and did a couple of jumping jacks to relieve the tension. His heart was pounding, and his palms were sweaty almost as if they were already together and …. Daly leaned his two elbows on the back of his computer chair and took a few deep breaths to clear his head and slow his racing pulse.

When his breathing and heart rate were back in the normal range, he turned his attention to the here and now and his plan for the day. He needed to attend to his online ladies and replenish his bank account. That was another result of the recent unfortunate turn of events. It had played hell with his income and therefore his bank account. A man can't live without money, and bless their stupid little desperate hearts, there were so many little phishes out there, ready and willing him to send him as much money as he needed.

The problem was keeping them all straight. One wrong move, use one wrong name, get one fact wrong, and the whole thing could go sour, and all that careful work would be forever lost. Right now, the fear of making a mistake was rendering him more likely than ever to make one.

Not that anyone would ever be able to learn his real identity; he was way too good for that to happen. But if one of his online darlings caught him in a misstep and started asking questions, or if he mixed up a date or a reference, the money would stop, and a man has to pay his bills, doesn't he?

He knew that once he managed to get everything back on track, so to speak, he wouldn't be so agitated, but until then, and from now on, he needed to be hypervigilant. Having a firm date for the new # 2 on the dark list would go a long way to easing his inner tension.

He was startled to hear something outside his door. The cat? His landlady? No, she'd knock. He opened the door and found an envelope on the little table outside his door. It was an invitation to have tea by the fire with everyone at 4:00 on New Year's Day afternoon. That's nice of her, he thought and made a note-to-self to get a bouquet of flowers —no, make that a box of some kind of imported chocolates and a bottle of champagne. He would hand write his acceptance, as he had been taught. My God, he thought, how long ago was that?

Years back in another life time, he'd worked for the government, doing much the same kind of top-secret undercover work he was doing now, except he did it for a legitimate, taxable salary. He'd constructed different personae and found out-of-the-way places to live so he could do his work and not attract attention. But there was no way in hell that he or anyone else in the field could have constructed such a perfect cover as he had right now. Those days were long gone. Only the shame of being removed from his position lingered on, removed because he'd made another stupid mistake. The memory made him still shiver, but that was then, and this was now. He pulled himself into the present and congratulated himself on his nearly fool-proof living situation.

Perfect houseguest, meet perfect gullible landlady, geeky sister, and blinded by love Irish cop. Why thank you, sir/madam, delighted, I'm sure. Would you care for another cup of tea? Talk about the luck of the Irish. You haven't lost your touch, Daly, you've still got what it takes. He chuckled all the way to his little bathroom.

Later, back in his room, he wrote a quick note to Viridienne, accepting her kind invitation for Tea at 4:00 on New Year's Day afternoon, and left it for her on the front stairway.

Kevin didn't grow up in a house with a front and back stairway, one for the family and their guests and one for the servants. He only knew that such things existed, and they weren't for the likes of him.

Meanwhile, he had work to do. First off, he needed to attend to his ladies and his steady income, then he needed to find himself something to do and somewhere to do it on New Year's Eve. Staying home alone and playing video games was not an option. Isolation and depression were his constant companions. Getting outside and moving around in the fresh air, no matter how cold, released some of the inner tensions and helped him keep the compulsions under control.

By the time he finished connecting and further milking his income ladies, he had a plan for New Year's Eve. He told Viridienne in a text that he would be spending the night in downtown Boston and would be back home the following day in plenty of time to enjoy afternoon tea with them all.

55

By the afternoon of December 31st, Fitz and Viridienne also had a plan for the evening. Despite the fact that Fitz and Alison were making serious inroads on the current investigation, even detectives need a break. Their evening would include no talk of work, online boyfriends, upcoming art shows, the price of fish or national politics. Even detectives deserved down time. He planned to work a half-day, go home and spend some time with his mother, and then head over to Viridienne's house. There the two of them, and of course Emily, would consider which take-out establishment to honor with their custom and make the appropriate phone call or calls, depending on who wanted what. When the heady repast was delivered, Viridienne would light the candles, Emily would set out paper plates and cutlery and, of course, the very best second-hand-store, polished crystal and only slightly chipped, champagne flutes.

At the appointed hour Fitz would pour the champagne, and they would all sit down together at the dining room table. After that, if they weren't already floating dimly in a self-inflicted food coma, they would repair to the sitting room, enjoy the last night of the Christmas tree, and play a game or two of Scrabble in front of the fire. Finally, they would finish off the evening with heaping bowls of English trifle topped with real whipped cream, something Viridienne had been dying to make ever since she'd read about it in an English detective story.

There was one more delight planned for that evening, and it did not include Emily or Scrabble or trifle. It was left unspoken and only discreetly acknowledged in pink-cheeked smiles and knowing looks.

That same afternoon Kevin Daly was driving up Route 3 toward Boston. He knew exactly what he was looking for, and he knew exactly where to find it. That morning he'd booked a room online in a chain hotel as close to Boston's trendy and gaily fashionable South End as he could. He planned to leave his car at a transit sponsored parking lot and, much as he loathed it, use public transportation to take him where he needed to go and back.

Some days after that one or two people who lived and partied in that particular corner of Boston's reclaimed brownstone neighborhood would ask about the guy who had come into The Rainbow Lounge dressed to the nines in a navy-blue tuxedo. They all remembered he had a flower in his buttonhole and a nasty scar on his face. Some remembered he had bushy eyebrows. Others thought he was carrying something. Strange, really, they said, for someone who clearly liked to dress like that not to do something about those eyebrows. They really detracted from the image. And who the hell carries a briefcase into a bar on New Year's Eve?

Not from around here, they said. But then, nobody saw

him leave the place either, and that was weird, wasn't it, because he was not a guy you'd forget. By the end of the week, it would be old news and any curiosity about him replaced with concerns about the homeless man found lying dead in a trash-filled alley the next day. But before long, that too was old news. "He musta froze to death. Cold as a witch's tit that night," someone commented.

"Or a well-used, well-diggers arse," joked his friend.

56

On the morning of New Year's Day, the three residents of La Vie en Rose slept in, not because they were hung over, but because they could. This time Fitz didn't feel the need to slither out the door in the early morning before anyone saw him. Instead, fully dressed and shaven, he joined the two women who were still in their bathrobes, sat down for breakfast and looked at neither of them.

"I suppose I should have thought to mention it last night, but I can make the best scones you ever did taste. Family recipe. Would you two like that?

"What's a scone?" asked Emily. She pronounced it with a long "o" to rhyme with stone.

Fitz held up an index finger. "A scone, has a short 'o' like in pond or bond or font. Think of it as not having that final 'e.' at the end. But in the long run, a scone is a scone no matter how you say it, and it is usually had with afternoon tea, but we Irish have been known to make exceptions."

"What do we need?" asked Viridienne.

He listed the ingredients. "Flour, butter, light cream, if you have it, baking powder, a touch of sugar, some dried cranberries or raisins, if you fancy them, and of course, a big black cast iron skillet to bake them in. That's a must." He paused. "Well, according to my gran, it was."

"Done deal, said Viridienne, hopping up out of her chair and heading for the pantry. Emily went after the mixing bowl and the skillet, and before long Fitz went to work while the women looked on in awe and anticipation.

"We Irishmen are not typically known for our kitchen skills, but I do have a couple of real treasures tucked away up here." He pointed a floury finger at his temple. "It's not all corned beef, beer and boiled potatoes. A lot of it is, but not all of it."

He talked them through each step of what he was doing and before long set a platter of hot cranberry and raisin scones with a soft "o" on the table in front of them.

"We need some butter and jam," he said, then added. "If I'd thought about it, I'd have tried to find us some clotted cream, but that's really for high tea in the afternoon." He turned and winked conspiratorially at Viridienne. "Stick with me, woman. I'm not just a pretty face, don't' ya know. There's more t'me than meets yer ... grey-green eyes."

Viridienne blushed and looked down at the scones. Emily blushed and busied herself doing something noisy at the sink. Fitz grinned even more broadly than before. He had all the appearances of a very happy man.

AT EXACTLY FOUR in the afternoon, Kevin Daly emerged

from his room armed with a bottle of notable champagne (chilled!) and a sizeable box of imported chocolates and made his way to the La Vie en Rose sitting room to join the others. To say he looked like something that even the cat wouldn't drag in was an understatement. The man looked like hell. His face was scratched, and he had a swollen and darkening left eye.

Before anyone could ask or look away, he held up his right hand and said, "Note to self. Don't have one too many and take the short cut you think you remember back to your hotel. What you see here is courtesy of a dark alley, a bramble bush, an abandoned shopping cart and exceedingly poor judgment. I can assure you and myself that it will not happen again." He took a mock bow and Viridienne, shaking her head in sympathy, directed him to an empty chair.

"I'm not proud of myself," he added, "but it's all surface damage. It will fade, and I have learned a tough lesson, and that's all that need be said." He held up the champagne and pointed to the chocolates. "Let's change the subject. Do you have some glasses we might use for this stuff, Viridienne?"

After a few awkward attempts at kindling a conversation, only to have it sputter out, Emily raised her glass and said, "Let's drink to the New Year, and then each of us can tell the rest of us, if we've made a resolution for the coming year, what it is."

"Do we have to tell the truth?" asked Fitz. "You know the Irish are famous for their storytelling. "Will any of us know?" quipped Viridienne with a Cheshire cat grin.

Fitz continued, undaunted, and turned toward Kevin. "You're Irish, aren't you? I mean with a name like Kevin Daly you have to be."

"Right in one," said Kevin with a tight smile, but he said no more.

"Well, my resolution is that I am going to go out on a real date," said Emily, "my first ever."

Viridienne flicked a warning glance in Fitz's direction but said nothing.

"What about you, Viridienne?" asked Fitz.

"I want to do something to make a difference."

"What kind of a difference?" Emily cocked her head and looked at her sister.

"Ask me that next year, and I'll tell you if I did. Meanwhile, there are some take-out leftovers just waiting to be heated up. Dinner in our laps and a movie is the plan for the evening, and for dessert, if you're really good and clean your plates, I'll let you help me take down the tree."

With that, Viridienne and Emily scampered off toward the kitchen, leaving Fitz and Kevin staring into the fire.

"We're a great pair, then, wouldn't you say?" said the detective. "Two Irishmen with a bottle between them and nothing to say. That has to be a first." He half snorted, half laughed, and soldiered on. "I spent a little time with my mother today before coming here. She loves me to take her to church. Your folks live nearby?"

"My father's been gone for years, and my mother lives in southern Maine. I try and get to see her a couple of times a year. It's complicated." He shrugged and left it at that.

Fitz raised both hands in surrender. "Family …"

The conversation, such as it was, was mercifully interrupted by Viridienne's call to come and get their dinner.

57

The next day Viridienne was vacuuming the carpet in the hallway outside Kevin's room, and she could still smell cat pee, not exactly an auspicious symbol of good fortune for the coming year. Even if Daly didn't seem to mind or even notice it, it would never do for a future guest. She stopped pushing and pulling the grumbling machine, switched if off and leaned on the handle. What to do?

She didn't want to sound like a scolding mommy and ask Kevin to re-do the job, especially after he'd brought them that really good Champagne and the chocolates to welcome the New Year. On the other hand, this was a class establishment, and upscale B&B's do not smell of cat.

Finally, setting aside her promises never to go into his room unannounced or unattended, she made the decision to wait until he was out, do the job as fast as she could and say nothing. If there was still a damp spot on the rug inside the door when he returned, she'd tell him a partial truth. She would say she could still smell it and had gone ahead and tackled it one more time from the outside. Any moisture and the smell of the cleaning solution must have wicked through from when she was cleaning.

Now all she needed was to watch for a time when the car was gone and then fly in there, touch nothing and get it over as quickly as possible. Viridienne was a woman of her word, and she didn't like breaking it; but if no one knew, and it was done in the line of duty, so to speak, and not snooping? So why did she feel so anxious, especially now that she was finally beginning to truly relax around the man.

Hadn't they all, including Fitz, sat together, knee to knee around the fire and raised a glass to the days to come? Hadn't they all, including Daly, told stories, pondered resolutions for the New Year and raised a second glass to the future that awaited them? So why did she feel so anxious, so guilty?

Whatever it was, she pushed it aside. Needs must, and cat pee is not acceptable. Now all she needed was the opportunity.

58

The opportunity to have a second run at the dreaded cat pee came the very next day. Kevin sent a text in early morning telling Viridienne he'd be out of town for the next two nights on business, and he didn't want her to think that his absence meant he'd scarpered off without paying the rent. He closed with two smiley faces and the word "joke" in parentheses.

She texted back a quick, "Thanks for letting me know, Kevin. Stay safe and keep warm. 😉."

Now ALL SHE had to do was wait for him to leave and tack on another hour or two to make sure he didn't come back because he'd forgotten something. Then, with no chance of being found out, she could tackle Project Pee. But now she would finish her breakfast, check her email and, because nobody had volunteered to help her the night before, she would take down the Christmas tree, a sweet-sad task. Nothing is sadder than a dried-out, drooping, needle-shedding, past its sell-by date Christmas tree. It had served them well, and it was time for it to go.

SHE'D ALREADY WON the argument with her conscience about going into Kevin's room, so she decided to get it over and done with and get the aggravation out of her mind. The tree could wait. It wasn't going anywhere. When her chores were finished, she would reward herself with a deliciously hot shower and use her special hand-made herbal soap she saved for special occasions.

Still, she was uneasy as she approached the door with a master key in one hand and a bucket filled with cleaning tools and spray bottles in the other. Once inside, looking neither left nor right, she took a deep breath, dropped to her hands and knees and focused on the task at hand. She dug in and went to work just inside the door slowly working her way backward on her hands and knees. In minutes she had a rhythm going; spray, scrub-rinse-blot-dry-repeat; crawl back a couple of inches and continue the process.

She was almost finished, having backed up for the last swipe of the task, when she banged butt-first into the desk and heard Kevin Daly's computer wake up and *ding* into action. He'd obviously not powered it down before he left, and the impact of the rear-end collision jiggled the mouse just enough to activate the screen. At first, she panicked. Then, as much as she knew she shouldn't but in full assurance that he was well out of town, she gave into temptation and pulled herself up onto her feet so she could have a look. On the open computer was what appeared to be a letter. Who would know?

She leaned down, taking care not to rest her hands on the desk and leave palm prints on the polished surface, and read the words on the screen. It was a letter, all right. A letter telling the addressee, clearly a woman, that he was desperately sorry that things didn't work out this time, that his leave got cancelled, and he'd had to forfeit the money he'd spent on the tickets and the hotel room. He assured her that this was now and not forever, and he knew things would work out, that she just had to trust him. She did trust him, didn't she? Meanwhile, the airline and the hotel were both charging him cancellation fees, and he of course couldn't get at his money, so as much as he hated doing it, could he please impose on her generosity one more time so he could get this taken care of and not ruin his credit rating??? Pretty please. 😳 Think of all that's ahead of us??? Help me this one time …

By the time Viridienne finished reading, she was furious and visibly shaking but very much in control of her wits. She reached into her pocket for her cell phone and snapped a couple of pictures of the screen. Then, after a couple of deep breaths to steady herself, she removed every trace of her being there, tiptoed out of the room and looked the door. She knew the computer would go back to sleep all by itself, and so she confidently left it to its own devices.

She put away the cleaning things and made herself a cup of cocoa. She thought seriously about adding a shot of rum to it but instantly thought better of it.

Of course, she needed to show this to Fitz, but then what? Confront the man? Evict him? On what grounds? Admit she was snooping? On the other hand, what if it was legit? What if Daly had a girlfriend somewhere, and they had plans, and something in his business popped up and blew it all out of the water? Consultants and other people who work for themselves have to go where the money and the work is, or they don't stay in business for very long.

But you don't know that for sure, do you, Viridienne? She wasn't doing a very good job of convincing herself. She took a long, self-indulgent sip of her cocoa and reached for one of the remaining chocolates. But you do know someone who can give you a second opinion, she reminded herself. She pulled out her phone, texted the pictures along with a clarifying note and a string of question marks to Fitz. Sometime back he'd given her a private emergency number, but to her thinking, this might be highly question-able, but it wasn't a life-threatening emergency. It could be something, and it could be nothing, and Fitz, bless him, was the man to ask. She texted him on his regular number.

For the time being anyway, she would say nothing to Emily. Had she not just recently warned her sister about this very thing? Considering she was now hyper-sensitive on the subject of sisterly supervision; discretion would defi-nitely be the better part of valor. She would ask Fitz and then follow his advice. But right now, she would calm her nerves by finishing her cocoa and persuading herself to eat one more chocolate.

WHEN VIRIDIENNE'S text came through, Fitz lifted his phone off the desk and looked at caller ID and saw she'd sent a couple of screen-shots. Clearly, she wanted him to look at something. He gave it a quick glance. It appeared to be more social than business, so he shot back a TTYL (talk to you later) and planned to read it more fully when he and Alison took their next break. The two were working their way through a veritable sea of information pertaining to the current investigation.

Much of what was in front of them merely confirmed

what Fitz had already deduced for himself. The murders were always in threes, the victim was always a gay man, and the M.O. was the same for all of the crimes. Each set of three took place within the space of a few weeks and then radio silence, would you believe, for exactly three months. After that the whole deadly pattern would play itself out once again.

Now there was a ray of hope. It was almost certain Fitz had the suspect on the end of his phishing line. The print-out showed the repeated pattern of killings had been going on for almost two years. The first one took place on the west coast. After that the killer worked his way across the country. If the local murder on South Point and the attempted murder had been perpetrated by the same man, and there was every indication that they had been, Fitz could be the man to take him down and put an end to the savagery for good. Please, God, let me be successful, he thought. If he failed, the killer would continue working his heinous way back and forth across the country until he was caught or until another attempt backfired and he got killed himself.

Fitz looked over the pile of papers in front of him. "Alison?"

She looked up at him from the remains of a bagel and two empty coffee containers.

"Yes, Kemosabe."

"You do know that I have a date with my mystery man on January 6th. I would like you to be my shadow back-up. As far as we know, the man has never used a gun, so it's unlikely he carries one. He relies on shock, speed and practice."

Alison nodded, her face blank and her mouth flat. He knew that look. The woman could move like a cat when she needed to, quickly, silently and accurately. Among her many accomplishments was years of training in the martial arts.

"I suppose it's a stupid question, but do you know what he looks like? I mean, don't people exchange photographs on these sites?"

He shrugged. "I have a photo, but it could be anyone. These phishers take a random picture off the internet or copy it off Facebook and use it. Sometimes they'll even copy something off an obituary. They have no conscience. They're animals." He powered up his alternative tablet and opened the file.

"There. What do you think?"

"Not exactly clear, is it?"

"It could be him. It could be someone who sort of looks like him. The man does expect me to recognize him when we meet, so it can't be too far off. Most often guys, and women as well, will use a younger, thinner, more enticing picture of themselves on these things. On some of the gay men's sites, a lot of them don't even bother showing their face."

She grimaced. "Tell me about it."

Fitz laughed in spite of himself and the severity of the situation. "Uh, Sorry about that."

She threw up her hands. "Hey, it's all in a day's work. So give me the worksheet for date night. Do I present as a man or a woman?"

"Androgynous. I want you to look like a person who could be either. People will take less notice of you. Anyone looking at you will see what they want to see and forget it unless they decide to make a move on you."

"And then?"

"Alison, if there is anybody on God's green earth that

can rid themselves of a would-be suitor, it's you, I've seen you in action."

By way of response she crossed her two fists in front of her face, growled and announced, "I need a body-break. Can I have ten minutes off for good behavior?"

Fitz gestured toward the door. "Take your time. I need to go back over and check with my colleague, John Stokes, in forensics. He's a genius at this. But I still want to go over that clothing one more time and see if there's anything I might have missed. You know me, I'm a measure-twice, cut-once, kind of guy."

"AKA perfectionist," said Alison, pulling on her coat, "and the world is a safer place because of it." She paused and winked. "That's OK, Fitz, don't bother getting up. I'll see myself out."

He grunted, "Women!" and fired a wad of paper in her direction.

59

K evin Daly returned to the house earlier than was expected. He realized, with shot through the brain of cold fear, that he'd forgotten to turn off his computer. He slipped silently through the rear door and sat down at his desk. His movements, elbows on the desk, and pulling up his chair, were enough for the computer to spring into life, and his most recent apologetic begging letter flashed up onto the screen.

Fuck! I must have hit sleep instead of shut-down before I left. He was shaking in both fear and anger when the unmistakable smell of white vinegar told him someone had been in there. It could only have been Viridienne … Viridienne who was a bed-buddy of a cop who was doubtless trying to find him at this very minute.

Calm down and get rational, man. She's a decent person. She was after the cat pee. If you hadn't come back early, you never would have known. But did she look at the computer? And if she did, how much did she see?

He was pacing now, clenching his fists and hyperventilating. Get hold of yourself man…there's only one way to find out. Go out and confront her.

Daly dropped onto the bed and lay staring at the ceiling. He knew that he was far too agitated to think clearly and that would only lead to more slip-ups. He began slow deep breathing, forcing himself to count each inhale and exhale, thinking of nothing else but the breathing … but the thoughts kept slipping in. When they did, he tried to reason with them.

Why should he think Viridienne would be going through his things? He knew what suspicious people looked and acted like, knew the kinds of loaded questions they would ask. Didn't they drink his champagne and eat his chocolates together just the other day? She'd promised … but people break promises. He had to find out. The kid sister was not even a consideration. But the cop, he could be trouble.

Another long inhale, even slower this time. Concentrate on the breathing, man. Forget the cop. He's just a guy protecting his woman. He's nobody's fool, but the last place he's gonna look is under his own two feet. Breathe.

He was calming down and starting to think clearly, which meant confronting Viridienne and learning for himself what she'd done and what she'd seen when she went into his room after saying she would not—and why, after giving her word, had she gone back on her word?

Viridienne was in the kitchen, sitting at the table rereading the letter she'd taken off Daly's computer, trying to make sense of it. She really wanted to talk to Fitz about it but drew the line at calling him at work. What she'd found was troubling, but was it an emergency? Not likely.

If the letter was a straightforward exchange between two people, then so be it. And if Daly was one of those guys, the kind she'd only recently warned her sister about, then by alerting Fitz she will have been a contributing factor to getting one more slime bag off the internet. These guys weren't violent, as far as she knew—just despicable.

This got her to thinking about her sister and the idea of doing a little more nosing around the You-Me-We dating site. Maybe, sometime when Emily was out, she should log on to her computer and check it out for herself. They had each other's passwords, and while she didn't like the idea of spying on her sister, she simply could not get past the need to protect her. She leaned forward on her elbows and stared down at the phone.

"What's that you're looking at, Viridienne?"

Startled, she looked up to see Kevin Daly standing in the doorway.

60

Fitz was sitting, hunched over, at a long table. He was wearing a bulky sterile smock over his clothes and rubber gloves on his hands. Thus prepared, he was methodically going over every inch, stitch and seam, inside every pocket and cuff-fold of the blood-stained clothing and shred of the newspaper it came in. He was deeply engrossed when the "Irish Washer Woman" ring-tone interrupted his concentration. He considered letting it go to voice mail, because to look at it would mean un-gloving and re-gloving, an irritating task at best. Then he remembered he had a message from Viridienne that still needed a response. He grunted and fumbled through the layers of cloth and finally dug out the phone. It was a message from his mother, inviting him to supper. He quickly typed, "Rain-check, please?" to his mother and then tapped on Viridienne's name.

Along with three pictures of a computer screen were these words:

. . .

"HI FITZ, I found this by accident on Kevin Daly's computer today when he was out, and I wondered if it was something that needed your looking at? I'll be home all afternoon. V"

HE TOOK A QUICK LOOK. At first glance, it looked like a typical phisher-pitch, but it could just as well be a guy making lame excuses for something he screwed up. Whatever it was, if Viridienne thought he should look at it, then look at it he would. The woman was no fool, and he was only half kidding when he told her he could find work for her in criminal investigation, if she were interested. She definitely knew how to find things and had that crucial sixth sense, that intuitive knowing that made the difference between a first-class investigator and a rank and file worker-bee.

Reluctantly, he turned back to the task at hand and pulled on another pair of purple latex gloves. God, he hated the feel and the smell of these damn things.

61

"Oh, hi, Kevin. Sorry, you startled me. I didn't hear you come in. I wasn't expecting you until tomorrow. Everything all right? Would you like a cup of tea or coffee?"

The man walked around the table and sat down across from her. "I'm not thirsty, Viridienne, I'm deeply concerned over the fact that you went into my room while I was out."

The skin on the back of her neck began to prickle, and there was not one thing she could do about the pink tinge of embarrassment that was warming her cheeks.

He leaned forward, elbows on the table, and stared at her. His voice was cold and flat. "You went in there, didn't you? Even after you said you wouldn't. Why did you lie to me?" He stared at her. "I know you did, because I used the old hair-across-the-door trick. The hair was gone. Someone, no doubt you, opened the door to my room. I have one question. Why?"

"It … it was the cat pee," she stammered. "I could still smell it, and it bothered me. I didn't want that for you.

You're a good tenant." She kept her hands tightly folded on the table in front of her to keep from wringing or twisting them. "You said you'd be gone for a couple of days. I thought I had the time to get in there, get it cleaned up for good, and you'd never know." She looked back at him. "Was that really so wrong? I didn't touch anything. What I looked at was the floor and the carpet around the door. I couldn't even tell you if the bed was made or not. So yes, I did go into your room, but I did it with good intent and as a professional courtesy to you. I would do the same for any other guest of the establishment. I repeat, yes, I did go into your room, and I apologize. Will you accept my apology?"

He remained steely eyed. "You said you wouldn't go into my room, and I believed you. You lied."

This was going downhill fast. She tried a second time. "Kevin, I admitted that I did. I touched nothing, and I've apologized. What else can I say?"

"The computer was on when I came back."

The pink flush of embarrassment on her cheeks was rapidly darkening into the red of anger, and her voice was rising.

"The computer was on when you left, Kevin. I didn't touch it. If it was all that important, why didn't you take it with you?"

"That's not the point. How do you know it was on?"

"Kevin, I was crawling around on my hands and knees, scrubbing the rug for you! I accidentally backed into the desk and heard the computer wake up. I was surprised that you'd gone away and left it, but I did not turn it on or otherwise touch it in any way. Why would I?"

"I don't believe you."

"What?" Her voice was rising.

"I don't believe you. I think you went into my room and

dumped a little white vinegar around as false evidence. That way you could have a good old snoop for yourself. Tell me what else you found, Viridienne. No, better yet, tell me what you were looking for."

By now Viridienne was both furious and scared, but her years of practice at holding things in when she had been a captive child would serve her well now. She chose her words with surgical precision.

"Kevin, I will not allow you to accuse me of wrong-doing in my own home. Yes, I went into your room against your wishes, but I went in to clean it and make it nicer for you. I did not have an ulterior motive. If you don't believe me, and I can't convince you otherwise, I think it might be best for all concerned that you find another place to live. I will dissolve the lease and refund any money that is due to you, and we can go our separate ways."

By the look on his face and his rapid breathing, it was evident that he was not prepared for the response he got. He was a man who was used to being in control.

"Fine, then. If that's what you want, stay right there. I'll go get the folder with the lease in it, and we'll be done with it. I'll clear out my things right after that," he assured her.

"I'll wait here."

Daly wasn't prepared for that either. The stupid meddlesome woman had just called his bluff.

62

While Fitz was alone in the office, waiting for Alison to return, he pulled up the image that Viridienne had sent onto his primary computer in order to examine it more closely. He didn't often do personal business in the office, but it was the only way he could read the words in the screen shot right now and not later. When he did, his blood went cold and his blood pressure went from zero to one thousand in the time it took to say, "Jaysus, Mary and Joseph."

At the very end of the letter were the words he'd been looking for in the murder investigation: "Don't be sad, just be patient with me. We've got our whole lives ahead of us …we can make it happen. Love always, DW"

There it was, "…we can make it happen." The format, the spacing, the sentence length, the predictable visual pattern on the page, it was all there in front of him.

Fitz had his man, and he was living in Viridienne's house, in his beloved Lady Greensleeves' house. He himself had broken bread with the man, joked about being Irish, bent elbows together. "Shit!" he roared again and again into the empty room, all the while pulling on his jacket and bolting for the door.

He knew that beating himself up for being taken in would do no good at all. This guy was a pro. Guilt and shame would mess with his thinking, and that was the last thing Fitz needed. Just get on with it, he told himself. The man was obviously a master at deception.

And he was within arm's reach.

His next thought was to get to Viridienne's house as fast as he could. He knew Daly was out of town. He'd said so himself on New Year's Day. He had time. He needed to get Viridienne and her sister out of there and settled some-where. Then he would stake the place out and wait, coiled like a cobra, for Kevin Daly to return. He pushed down on the gas pedal and quickly came to a screeching halt at a flagman in front of a bright orange detour sign.

To his mounting concern, he learned that the local gas company was chasing a reported leak and had torn up half of Court Street in the process. Even the flashing lights, which he did not want to use, wouldn't get him through any faster. He had time. Daly was out of town, he said so himself. Please God don't let him come back early.

Drumming his fingers on the steering wheel didn't help, but it did keep Fitz from punching his fist through the windshield.

63

I t was less than five minutes from the time that Daly stormed out of the kitchen until she heard him walking slowly back. Viridienne was standing beside the sink when he came through the door, carrying a manila folder with the words Rental Agreement written across the front. He slapped it onto the table and pulled a pen out of his shirt pocket.

"There! Let's make this happen, the sooner the better."

Viridienne walked over to the table and opened the folder.

"Why don't you sit down? I'm not going to bite you. You're so damn tall you probably can't read it from up there. I just want to get this the fuck over with."

Viridienne shook her head. Being as tall as she was had its advantages. She picked up the folder and opened it, only to have the papers slide out and cascade all over the floor. Instinctively, she bent over to pick them up, and when she did, Daly was on her like a panther. Dark, fast and lethal, in one motion he knocked her off balance and went for her throat.

The next few seconds were a hideous blur. Viridienne twisted and screamed and tried to push him off, but her own scream was lost in another scream and then another, and Daly was on the floor. He was howling in pain and clawing at the orange hairball of fury who, with a mighty tomcat screech of his own, launched himself off the top of the fridge and caught Daly with all twenty claws square in the face.

Fitz was standing in the doorway with his gun pointed at Daly. "Get the cat, Viridienne. Daly, you are under arrest on suspicion of the murder of David Nevins, assault with intent to kill of Winslow Bishop, Viridienne Greene and God-only knows how many more." He paused for breath. "Get to your feet. Now."

"I'm bleeding, I can't see. Fucking godddam cat. It attacked me."

"Watch your language."

By now Viridienne had a stiff-legged DT in her arms and was trying her best to calm and quiet him, but the cat was having none of it. It was clear from his low insistent growl that he wanted nothing more than to finish the job he'd started.

Fitz, his gun still trained on Daly, was calling for back-up. He sidestepped around the man on the floor, then handed him the paper towel roll that Viridienne kept beside the sink.

"And wipe up the spots on the floor while you're at it," he growled.

Viridienne looked over the top of her tough old one-eyed cat at the man she loved. She knew that now. Not because he'd just saved her life for a second time that year;

that was only part of it. But she would hold that thought. Her kitchen was a crime scene, and the police cars were flashing and screaming toward them. This was not how she had envisioned her life as the owner-manager of a genteel B&B, but what was that vision, and was it changing? She would hold on to that thought as well.

"Vid? Are you all right? Fitz! Oh my God. Is that a real gun?" Emily looked across the room at the shredded remains of Kevin Daly's face. "Vid, Fitz…what's going on? Kevin, you're hurt."

"I have just arrested this man on suspicion of murder, attempted murder, false impersonation with intent to commit a crime, and operating an internet scam," Fitz informed her.

"He's bleeding," wailed Emily.

"I know," said Fitz, his face twisted in disgust, "and it's going to be downhill from here. Kevin Daly, or whatever the hell your real name is, get up off the floor. The nice young men in their pretty blue suits are coming to arrest you." He paused, fighting for control. "God help us all."

As the arresting officer, Fitz was required to go with the uniformed police officers and their captive to station headquarters. Needless to say, every light in every window in every house in the neighborhood was on, and everyone who was at home was looking out their windows at the unfolding drama.

Viridienne and Emily, holding onto each other, stood on the front porch and watched until the police and Daly were gone, and all was quiet. Shivering from both the cold and what had just taken place in their own kitchen, they turned back into the house and pulled the door shut behind them.

"What happened, Vid?"

"All hell just broke loose, and it broke loose right here in our own house. Right here," she pounded on the table. "That man was going to kill me, right here in my own kitchen. If it hadn't been for DT …"

Emily put her arms around her sister. "Sit down, Vid." She began rubbing her older sister's back and shoulders, comforting and soothing her as you would a frightened hysterical child.

"You're okay now. He's gone and done. First off, I want you to have a big glass of water, and then I'm going to make us something hot. How does that sound?"

Viridienne nodded, calmer now but still shaking.

"Do you remember when Fitz showed us how to make an Irish coffee? How about one of those? No, make that two. It has coffee and whiskey. It will wake you up and calm you down at the same time, and I think we still have some of those fancy chocolates." Em stopped short and shook her head. "Uh, no. On second thought, not those."

"How about a Tiramisu Irish coffee?" Viridienne was coming back into her own skin.

Emily cocked her head to one side. "What's that?"

"I just invented it. Coffee, whipped cream, whiskey, chocolate syrup, a splash of brandy, and we dust some cocoa powder on top. Maybe add a little cinnamon."

"How about some glitter?"

"Oh, no, that would be gilding the lily, and we can't have that."

The tension in the room was dissolving, the evil shadows were in retreat, and the two women, who were still getting to know each other, were getting silly in their shared relief.

"Allow me to do the honors, big sister, you need some

TLC. God knows you've been looking after me for long enough. Now it's my turn. You wipe off the table and get out the tall glass coffee mugs. I'll take care of the rest. Then, when we are duly fortified, I want you to tell me, word for word, what just happened."

"Thanks, Em." Viridienne wiped her eyes and blew her nose. "To be honest, I don't know how we came to have a serial murderer living under our own roof and how Kevin Daly, or whoever he is, has made fools of us all."

At the sound of the man's name, DT, who was sticking to Viridienne like Velcro, began the low murderous growl that had been crucial in saving his lady's life.

"And you, you one-eyed wonder and protector of the realm, you are going to get a whole slab of perfectly cooked salmon, butter, no lemon, all for yourself. And a dish of vanilla ice cream after that."

WHEN FITZ CALLED to check on the two women and tell them that he and the forensic crew would be back to secure the room for the night, the sisters were still sitting at the table decompressing. "The team will come back tomorrow," Fitz told Viridienne, "and go through everything in there and collect anything they feel might be used as evidence."

"I feel like the room is contaminated," said Viridienne after she disconnected the call. She and Em were starting on their second Tiramisu Irish coffees.

"I want to have it fumigated the way you do if you have rats or something dies in there."

"Let the professionals come in and do their work," said Emily. "Once they're finished in there, we can go in and get rid of anything they don't take. Then we hire a professional cleaning service to literally sterilize the place. After that we can rename it and have fun recreating it."

"That should do it." Viridienne raised her cup in her sister's direction. "And I think I don't need to finish this. It's done its work. Fitz can fill in the blanks when he comes back."

Emily collected the two mugs, carried them to the sink, emptied them and turned to her sister. "I don't know about you, Vid, but I need a good long walk in cold fresh air. I need to blow out the cobwebs."

"Excellent idea. I'll go get my coat." She held up a finger as she was wont to do when making a point. "When we get back, we're going to turn off the heat and open every door and window in every room of this house, top to bottom, and let some of that cold fresh air get the stink out of this place as well."

64

B reaking News: **Suspected Serial Killer Arrested in Downtown Plymouth**
Yesterday Geoffrey Bryce, known locally as Kevin Daly, was arrested on multiple charges and placed without bail in the Plymouth County House of Correction. It is suspected that this man may be connected to a string of murders and assaults of gay men which have occurred across the country over the last two years. A hearing is scheduled for Monday, after which further details will be made available.

65

At about seven in the evening, Fitz called to say he'd like to come over and see how they were doing after all that had befallen them and go over the procedure for the following day with the forensic team.

"Please do," was Viridienne's instant response. She was still very shaken by what had happened. She was hoping that Fitz could provide some badly needed answers to her mountain of questions. That, and she found herself to be in desperate need of the feeling of safety and security that seemed to come in through the door with him.

"Do you need me to pick anything up on the way?" he asked. "Have you had your supper?"

"Neither of us is really hungry. We picked at some leftovers, but we've no real stomach for food just now."

"I'll be there within the hour."

And he was. With an oversized pizza box in one hand and a brown paper shopping bag in the other, he had to tap on the door with his foot.

As anyone who has ever had a hot pizza delivered to the

door will tell you, the heady smell of an everything pizza—the garlic, the cheese, essence of tomato overlaying hints of basil, green pepper, and oregano—would wake the dead. Viridienne felt her stomach, her taste buds and her brain spring into action.

"What's in the other bag?" she asked, already salivating as she pulled out the paper plates and set a roll of paper towels on the table.

Fitz began pulling items out and listing them. "Ice cream, chocolate syrup, Oreos, and ginger ale. All the things my mother gave to me when I was little and feeling poorly."

"Comfort food," said Viridienne.

"And it works," said Fitz, pulling open the pizza box. "Dig in, my ladies. Get it while it's hot."

LATER ON, in the tree-less and recently undecorated sitting room, the three sat with bowls of ice cream around the fire. For a while nothing could be heard but the clinking of spoons and the sound of a happy cat, purring loudly and making short work of his own bowl of ice cream.

"He's earned his keep, that one," said Fitz, setting his spoon into his empty bowl and patting his mouth with a square of paper towel. "DT, you deserve a medal of honor, or at the very least, you should be made an honorary member of Plymouth's finest."

"Fitz," said Viridienne, "Before you get into telling us what you can about Kevin Daly, I need to know what in the world got you here exactly when you did?"

"You did."

She gave him a curious look.

"I was already on my way over here when you hit the emergency call number I gave you. Only two people have it. Correction, three. You and my mother, and when Winn Bishop got out of the hospital, I gave it to him. You each have different rings. When I heard yours, I was stuck in traffic. I was already on my way here to find out about the images you sent me earlier. I hadn't been able to really go over them when they first came in because I was up to my eyeballs in forensics. But once I did, I knew I had to get over here and check it out. I wasn't in a huge hurry, though, because Daly had told us both he was going to be out of town for a couple of days, and then you hit the panic button."

Viridienne interrupted. "He came back. He'd forgotten his computer. When he realized he'd left it on, he decided I must have seen what was on it. He accused me of spying on him. After that, it got really ugly, really fast."

"But you weren't really spying on him, were you?"

"No, I was in there cleaning up the cat pee and I backed into his desk. It was just enough to jiggle the computer back to life."

"And then you looked."

She nodded. "I'm human."

"Bejayzuz you are, woman, and the world is a safer place tonight because of it, Viridienne Greene. My Lady Greensleeves. And you damn near got yourself killed in the process. That's one hell of a cat you've got there, with his one eye and all."

"You know what? Now that I think about it, from what you said, that cat never liked Daly."

"I'm not surprised. Animals pick up things long before we do. We've got a dog on the force. That damn thing can do everything but drive a car. He's brilliant."

"You still haven't answered my question. Here I am, all alone with a murderer. I'm in fear of my life, the cat has just defaced my attacker, and you walk in with a gun just in time to save my life."

Fitz chuckled. "Sorry, Vid, it's hardly funny, but in weird way, it kind of is. I was on my way here, and traffic was at a standstill courtesy of the local gas company looking for a reported leak. I'm stuck, hemmed in on all four sides when I hear your private ring on the emergency line. I had two choices. Abandon the car and run like hell or switch on the lights and the noise and plow through. I chose lights and noise, but I shut them off once I broke free. The last thing I wanted to do was alert Daly."

"How did you know he was here?"

"Ask the cat. Intuition. A sixth sense born of experience. You'd never used the emergency number before." He paused. "And you tell me, how did you manage to do it, without him finding out? He was standing there. If my memory serves me, you are an expert at sending messages in extreme situations. How'd you do it this time?"

"My phone was on when he came into the kitchen. When he left to get the rental agreement, the situation was tense, but considering the nature of the conversation, you'd expect that. I had no feeling of being threatened, just uncomfortable. It was only when he got back that I realized things had taken a very bad turn. He had a look on his face I'd never seen before, and it scared the hell out of me. I still had the phone in my hand, and when I reached for the folder and dropped the contents all over the floor, I used the distraction to alert you. All I could do was hit the button and beep and hope you'd get the message that I was in trouble." She looked up and smiled at her tough-tender Irishman. "Thanks, Fitz."

"What's going to happen to Kevin?" asked Emily.

"In a word, everything that can happen to a monster like that. We don't have a death penalty in this state. I'm against it anyway. But other states and other families are going to want to get their hands on him. I wouldn't be surprised if the defense tries to use an insanity plea, but that's not going to fly. He hasn't got a prayer."

Fitz changed direction. "So tomorrow morning, John Stokes, Anthony Hendryx, the photographer, and rest of the team will come over and go over everything in his room and remove what they need. They'll arrive bright and early and get right to work, so if you don't mind, I'd prefer to stay the night so I'll be up and dressed and ready when they arrive."

"Oh please, stay," said Emily. "I'd feel so much better with you here. I don't mind telling you, I'm a mess. I only I came in at the end of it all, but I came in early enough to see a man who'd just attacked my sister, sitting on the floor covered in blood and yelling for help. DT was howling and growling. You're standing there holding a gun on the guy, and my sister is shaking all over. Yes, Fitz, please stay here tonight."

"Do I have any say in the matter?" Viridienne, now almost fully back into her own body and mind, had an impish grin on her face.

"Not really," said her sister. "I'm inviting him. He can sleep where he wants. God knows we've got enough rooms."

66

Kevin Daly was in jail awaiting trial in Plymouth, Massachusetts. Pending the completion of that, several states across the country had filed petitions of extradition because they had active cases against him. But all of that was in the hands of the legal, prosecutorial and justice systems. What really mattered was that the man was permanently out of business. While Viridienne, Fitz and possibly even Emily would likely be called to testify, to all intents and purposes, the matter was history, and as such, out of their collective hands.

What still remained were bad memories, flashbacks and the need for peace and quiet at La Vie en Rose. Along with that would be the ritual purge of the back bedroom and everything in it. Emily and Viridienne were looking forward to that. When every trace of the man was gone, when the walls were a new color, the drapes different, and even the furniture, all of it, replaced, they would feel whole again and declare the establishment open for business. Until then it would remain closed.

Parallel to all of this, Fitz and Viridienne were growing and deepening their relationship. Add to that, Emily was still corresponding with Joe Franklin, the shadowy serviceman who would soon become a tangible reality as Valentine's Day fast approached—if he actually showed up. He'd not asked for any more money. Without Emily's knowledge, Viridienne and Fitz had done an internet search with the information she had given them—his name, his parents' names, place and date of birth, his date of entering the Navy—and it all checked out. They stopped short of calling Franklin's parents, but unbeknownst to Vid and Emily, Fitz ran a check on the family through his police connections with verifiable and acceptable results. These days, you can't be too careful.

Still, after the coming and going of Kevin Daly, a positive evil genius at multiple, alternate and false identities, the two remained quietly cautious about the whole thing, Emily remained quietly optimistic.

On the day before Valentine's Day, and after many breathless electronic conversations, Joe Franklin and Emily Rose Spencer had arranged that he would pick her up at home, come in and meet her sister and Fitz, and go out for dinner. On the appointed evening at the appointed time, a car pulled up in front of the house, and a man wearing a Navy officer's uniform walked to the door. No one could prepare him for what happened after that.

Emily opened the door with Viridienne and Fitz standing close behind, and upon seeing the man for the first time, all three of them burst into shrieks of laughter. He was carrying a bouquet of flowers in one hand and a box of chocolates in the other and looked totally nonplussed at the quality and volume of his reception.

When she could catch her breath, Emily said, "You

must be Joseph Franklin. I'm Emily. Please come in and get yourself out of the cold."

The young man took a backward step and said, "Is this some kind of a joke?"

Viridienne, who was now breathing normally, extended her hand and said, "Do come in, Joe. It's not a joke, but there is a story behind it, and I think you should hear it along with our collective apologies."

The man was not budging.

Emily tried. "It's okay, Joe, come on in. There's no way you could know this, but over Christmas, we had an … incident. We had a man living here who turned out to be a murderer. We didn't know that, of course. He was very charming, and he wasn't interested in murdering us, just gay men. The thing is, on several occasions, he showed up at the door with flowers and chocolate, and well, I think you get the picture."

Joe Franklin looked even more confused.

"Oh, never mind all of that," said Fitz. "Come in out of the cold, man. We're not all crazy here, it only looks and sounds that way. I think a cup of tea or a glass of wine, and perhaps some of those chocolates you have there, will go a long way to normalizing things."

Later, when Emily and her gentleman friend had left, Fitz and Viridienne were together in the kitchen, putting away the cups and the glassware. Fitz put down his dish towel and turned to Viridienne. "Vid, did I tell you my mother would like me to ask you to come for tea some Sunday afternoon?"

"She what?"

Fitz repeated the invitation. This would be a very big step; meeting the widowed mother, a retired professor of literature, who lived near but not with her only son. Am I ready for this? he asked herself. "Um, when was she thinking?"

She didn't want to say no because she didn't want to disappoint him and possibly ruin their future chances, but was she ready to say yes? She gave herself a mental shake. Viridienne, it's a goddamn cup of tea. It's not a formal dinner. Get hold of yourself.

"Tell her yes and thank you. I'd enjoy that very much."

67

S everal months later the dark chill of winter and the unkind winds of March were history in the town of Plymouth. Bright yellow and white daffodils planted along the walk front of La Vie en Rose were in full bloom and the forsythia along the side of the house was coming on fast. Spring, with its promise of new life, was in the air, and nowhere was evidence of new life as evident and as hopeful as inside the grand old Victorian house on Atherton Street. The back bedroom had been completely renovated, redecorated and renamed the Priscilla Mullins Room after a little girl who came over on the Mayflower in 1620. Later she would be poetically romanced and wed by John Alden and further immortalized by Henry Wadsworth Longfellow in his poem, "The Courtship of Miles Standish."

Breaking News-April 3

Geoffrey Bryce, AKA Kevin Daly and numerous other

aliases, has been officially accused of eleven counts of aggravated murder in the first degree, multiple charges of fraud, using false impersonation to commit theft, and two charges of assault with intent to kill. He is awaiting a trial in the Plymouth House of Correction.

68

By the first week in April, La Vie en Rose had several confirmed B&B bookings for the coming summer as well as an early one for the Easter weekend later that month. Business was picking up. It would appear that having a murderer for a tenant had done nothing to tarnish the reputation of the establishment itself and might even, because of the morbid curiosity factor of some, have benefitted it.

Viridienne, her sister Emily and Fitz, all wearing sweaters, were relaxing in the rocking chairs on the front porch. They were drinking in the bright midday sunshine and not quite warmth and noisy birdsong of early spring.

Emily was the first to speak. "I've decided to stop writing to Joe. He's nice enough, but he's not what I'm looking for."

Viridienne breathed out a long, slow and totally silent sigh of relief. "What brought that about, and does he know?"

Emily nodded. "He knows. Like I said, he's nice

enough, but that's it … nice. No fireworks. That, and since he's considering the military as a career, he'll always be on the move."

"Was he upset when you told him?" asked Fitz.

"Not really. We don't have a lot in common. We wished each other well."

"Fairly civilized, I'd say."

"No reason not to be. "We're good. He likes getting mail, so we'll probably keep writing for a while. I'm okay with that. I'm really not ready for any kind of commitment. I have way too much I want to do before that, if ever. I learned that, too. Having a boyfriend was nice, but it took up way too much time."

Viridienne and Fitz smiled and nodded in fond agreement.

"What about you, Lady Greensleeves, what's next on the docket for you? Or should I say, how's the B&B business shaping up for the season?"

"Funny you should ask."

"I'm not sure I like the sound of that."

"Would you believe I got a call just this morning asking if I would consider a two-month rental starting in May and going through to the end of June."

"What!" said Fitz and Emily simultaneously.

"You didn't accept it, did you? Emily's voice went up by a full octave. "We've just been through hell in a handbasket with one long-term renter. I hope you said no."

"No, I didn't say no. I said I'd get back to her, that I needed to think about it, which really means run it by you two."

"It's a woman then," said Fitz.

"Even better, she's a nun. She's a theologian who's doing post-doc work at Harvard Divinity School on the development of religious societies and congregations in colonial America as reflected and preserved in original town and church documents."

"This was not a casual conversation, then," said Fitz, "and to give the woman her due, a scholarly nun is hardly likely to pose a threat to the community."

"We trusted Kevin Daly, too, remember. Look what happened with him," said Emily.

Viridienne made a calming, slow down gesture in her sister's direction. "I talked to her, Em, then I went ahead and checked her credentials. She's quite the scholar. She's got several books to her credit, and she travels all over the world teaching and doing her research. I'd consider it an honor to have her here."

"And she's a Catholic, as well." Fitz was looking decidedly brighter. "There's hope for your wayward soul yet, my lady."

Viridienne gave him a playful smack on the arm. "She's an Anglican nun and she's from England. I love listening to her. It's like *Downton Abbey* revisited. She wants a place she can work from that isn't a motel. She'll be looking at original documents that go all the way back to the Mayflower Compact. She told me that some of these are kept at the Mayflower Society, in some of the records in the older churches and some in the museum. Plymouth is only her first stop. She is going to five more cities after this."

"Did you get her dress and shoe size as well?" quipped Fitz.

Viridienne rolled her eyes. "You may have guessed by now that I'm all for it, but out of courtesy, I'm asking you."

"Well, even if she is an Anglican, I say you can't get a much safer tenant than a nun."

"Okay, that's you, Fitz. Em?"

"As long as she doesn't spout religion at us, I'm in. I've had more than enough of that to last me two lifetimes."

"Well, then, I'll call her back and tell her yes. I think it's a good omen myself. She'll bring positive energy with her, and I hardly think we'll be needing your services on this one, my boy."

Fitz gave her a long look. "This nun, or no-nun, nonsense or none, count not your chickens before they are properly hatched, Lady Greensleeves, not even one."

Coda…
And the end of the day
I ask myself
Was it work, or play
Or both
Or just one giant cosmic glitch
Here by chance and gone…forthwith

To FIND other Olympia Brown Mysteries, click here, or www.UUA/Bookstore.org

They are also available in libraries, and if all else fails, contact the author at:

www.juithcampbell-holymysteries.com

THE MISSION MYSTERIES are also available on Amazon Audible.

SNEAK PEEK-A TWISTED MISSION

And now for something, not quite completely different, I invite you to read the **Olympia Brown Mysteries.** (12 in all) The protagonist is **Olympia Brown,** a lady minister with and eye and a nose for finding trouble in all the wrong places. From the first in the series, A Twisted Mission.

Chapter One

Without warning the snake slashed and zigzagged across the path just inches from his feet. He almost stepped on it. With his heart racing and sweat breaking out everywhere, he watched as the moving grasses off to his right indicated the direction of the reptile's speedy escape.

He straightened up and looked around to see if anyone had witnessed the incident but saw no one. He was morbidly afraid of snakes and had been since the day his father, drunk and trying to make a man of him, threw one in his face and then laughed when he screamed, fell on the ground and wet himself. The only thing he feared more than snakes these days was someone finding out about it. This was a close call, but so far his luck was holding. No one saw it. His shameful secret was still safe. When his breathing and heart rate returned to normal, he continued walking along the sandy path toward the crew shack. To be on the safe side, he stamped his feet, flapped his arms and made as much noise and commotion as he could.

Chapter Two

Across the street and up the short hill from the camp ground, a painfully thin and desperately unhappy young man scribbled a few words on a scrap of paper, folded it in half and pushed it deep into his jeans pocket. Then he climbed up on top of the battered old wooden dresser next to his bed. Careful to keep his balance, he tossed one end of a twisted sheet up and over the ceiling beam directly above him. He knotted it, yanked on it to test its strength and then secured it. Once that was done, he tied the other end around his neck. He had taken great care with the measurements so that when jumped off and kicked the shoddy dresser away from beneath him, his feet would not reach the floor. He hoped, even dared to pray, it would be quick.

Chapter Three

A fiftieth birthday, whatever else it might be, is a milestone. It can be a warning signal, a turning point or both. It can be loudly celebrated or quietly ignored, but it cannot be denied. It is a time when many will choose to step back and take stock. The Rev. Dr. Olympia Brown had just reached that significant event with as many questions in her mind as she had years logged onto the calendar. The two at the very top of the list were, should she continue as a college chaplain and professor of humanities and religion at Merriwether College, or should she change direction, leave academia and take on a full time parish ministry?

On the nonprofessional and more personal front there were more questions. Now that her two sons, Malcolm and Randall, were technically out of the safe suburban nest, her status as a not-very-swinging single was lonely. Maybe she should be more proactive about creating a little more action in that corner of her life. Maybe she should move out of her white, middle class, three-bedroom expanded cape in the town with the good schools that she needed when the boys were young and buy a condo in Boston or Cambridge. That would certainly ease her commute and save money on gas.

She could take her mother's advice, let nature take its course and wait for the universe to reveal what the future might offer—but Olympia rarely took her mother's advice, so she eliminated that one even before she wrote it down. And so it was on a spectacular summer day in early June, she was sitting in her back yard, sipping iced tea and making a list … or maybe it was a five-year plan—she hadn't decided which. In big block letters she created three columns across the top of the sheet of paper: Done, Yet to be done, and Wishful thinking bucket list.

If nothing else, and there was a whole lot of else, Olympia Brown was methodical and well organized. She typically set reasonable goals for herself and then in her own determined fashion strategized how to reach them. At age fifty, she knew who she was and pretty much what she wanted out of life. She also knew what she was and was not prepared give up in order to bring that about, or so she thought.

However, nothing that was about to happen in the coming summer was on this list and no one, not even Olympia, the practical plotter, could have predicted or planned for what did happen. She couldn't possibly know it, but it seemed she was at the mercy of a host of gods and goddesses who were bored and decided to have a bit of fun. The object of their ungodly mischief of fancy and foolishness was a middle-aged, slightly restless college professor who in one unguarded moment said she might be ready for a change. She looked again at the sheet of paper in her lap, made a face, and scrawled, "None of the above." Then she crumpled the paper and tossed back and high over her shoulder.

She decided to take a second look at the invitation she'd received to be a summer chaplain at Orchards Cove in Maine. A summer of fresh sea air and camping under towering pines in a seaside village would be a refreshing change and give her plenty of time to think about her future. Would it not?

Olympia's mother also told her, "Be careful what you wish for." It would have been good advice, had she listened, but she didn't, and therein hangs the tale.

If you'd like to read the rest of A Twisted Mission, click here.

AFTERWORD

"Ministry and murder are unlikely bedfellows," said Campbell, whose self-given nicknames include "the sinister minister," "irreverent reverend," and "perspicacious parson." "But put them together and they make for a good story and a good teaching tool."

My books address some pretty heavy topics. "What I do is hold up difficult issues for people to consider. I raise the questions, but I don't give the answers. It is a very different approach to writing a novel."

She presents writing workshops and Writing as Spiritual Practice workshops, for which she travels nationally and internationally, and shares poems, political satire, writing hints and ideas, and even recipes on her blog at judith-campbell-holymysteries.com.

Campbell says of her writing, "My words have work to do."

https://www.bostonglobe.com/metro/globelocal/2019/
09/11/minister-and-mystery-writer-explores-faith-through-
writing Cindy Cantrell, Boston Globe.

SNEAK PEEK, DOCUMENTARY EVIDENCE

And finally, a sneak peek into the next, *(third)* in the Viridienne Greene mystery series.

Documentarian, Sr. Benedicta Scholastica, AKA, Sister Bennie, is doing of post-doctoral work on the establishment and development of denominational Christianity in sixteenth and seventeenth century English and Spanish colonial America. Plymouth, Massachusetts, with its original and carefully preserved Mayflower and early settlement records, it is, without a doubt, the most logical place to begin her year of cross-country research.

On a bright day in late May, after an inquiring email, Sr. Bennie, turns up on the doorstep La Vie en Rose, wearing jeans and a sweatshirt, looking to book a room for the next eight weeks. She has with her, little more than a computer, and oversized backpack and she has parked a very second-hand car on the street in front of the house.

With good reason, Viridienne Greene is reluctant to take her in. The last person who requested a long-term rental, turned out to be a serial murderer of gay men, and a phishing con-man who made his living weaseling money out of lonely gullible women.

But in the end, her good references, plus a little internet research, *the woman really is a nun, with a solid academic and publishing record*, does the trick. That plus the fact that the intense, petite sister is also warm, funny and a bit of a scamp when no one is looking, sealed the deal.

She doesn't waste any time securing permission to access original documents from several churches, The Mayflower Society, Pilgrim Hall Museum, and the Archivist-Documentarian at Town Hall. To augment her research, she volunteers to work in the museum library, authenticating documents and repairing those that have suffered from the ravages of a damp salty New England sea-side climate. In so doing, she discovers a document, that only someone with her skills and expertise would know was forged. Expertly, beautifully…and almost perfectly forged.

Forged documents are a professional embarrassment and an insurance company fraud liability to/for the establishments/organizations that believe and present them to the public as real. They don't want to have someone point this out, and possibly take it to the press, especially if it's an intense little nun who they think can be easily intimidated. …They are dead wrong.

ENGLISH TRIFLE

(Mysteriously modified and magnified through use and experiment, by Judith Campbell.)

Trifle is a way for thrifty English and Irish people use up left-over cake…*if there ever is such a thing*…. Essentially, it's a giant parfait…made up of sequential layers of broken up of sliced cake, or lady fingers, or sponge cake,

You will need a clear glass bowl, (Actually, any big bowl will do, it's just that the trifle layers are pretty and should be seen. It adds to the all over experience!

Trifle recipe

Trifle is a way that thrifty English and Irish people use up left-over cake…if there ever is such a thing.

Essentially, it's a giant parfait…made up of sequential layers of:

broken up of sliced cake, or lady fingers, or sponge cake,

The size of the bowl, determines the amount of trifle, because the ingredients are according to taste and amounts available.

Start by covering the bottom of the bowl with a layer of broken up of sliced cake, or lady fingers, or sponge cake,

On top of that, add a layer of sliced fruit, strawberries, Canned, peaches or pears, blueberries, whatever you have

Onto this splash a liberal layer/ a good slosh of medium dry sherry (N.B. The sherry is optional, for those that don't use alcohol, but it is a traditional ingredient.)

And over it all, pour a layer of yellow custard, (Birds brand, instant custard…

or prepared vanilla pudding will do in a pinch.)

Repeat these layers once or twice until the bowl is almost filled and then cover with real whipped cream and possibly decorate with extra strawberries or raspberries.

Cover this with plastic wrap, or a clean plate, and set in the fridge for a couple of hours for the flavors to mix and mingle….and then prepare to swoon with pleasure when you eat it.

Easy awesome **LOW-CALORIE SCONES** (Pronounced, Scons.)

…also adapted by the author.

I think Poor Fitz would disapprove, but then he's a traditionalist, Whereas, I am a lazy opportunist when it comes to cooking. Fast, easy and delicious is my kitchen mantra.

preheat oven to 400 degrees f.

Ingredients

1 ½ cups Bisquick or store brand pancake mix or self - rising flour

2-3 tsp stevia (or to taste)

1-2 tbs cold butter

½ cup LOWFAT Greek plain or vanilla yogurt

¼-1/3 cup cold lowfat milk (Dough should just hold together and not be sticky.)

Directions

Cut butter into Bisquick or self-rising flour and dry stevia with a pastry cutter of the back of a fork until the whole mixture is crumbly.

Make a well in the middle of the mixture and plop in the yogurt and the milk and stir fast but not for very long.

If you are going to add raisins, craisins, dried fruits, now is the time. Do it quickly, don't over work the dough.

Turn the dough onto a non-stick (or greased) cookie sheet and bake at 400 degrees F. for 25-28 minutes… depending on your oven. Top and edges should be lightly browned, and the scones, springy to the tough.

Let cool, then serve with strong hot tea, butter and jam, clotted cream or sweetened cream cheese…and then sit back and wait for the shower of compliments.

NB. This is a basic recipe. You can flavor them with lemon zest, orange zest, ginger…or try cranberries and white chocolate. Of course, this takes it way out of the realm of low calorie…but you are the cook, and the choice is yours.

ABOUT THE AUTHOR

Rev. Dr. Judith Campbell is a community-based Unitarian Universalist minister. She has authored twelve books in the popular Olympia Brown Mystery series and has now started a second series, The Viridienne Greene Mysteries.

She has published poetry, children's books, two books on watercolor painting, and several articles on religion, spirituality, and the arts. She lives by the sea in Plymouth, Massachusetts, with her husband, Chris Stokes, along with their two cats.

Writing is her passion, her challenge, and the most authentic way she can live into her life and her ministry. What she attempts to do with her writing is to raise awareness around current social and ethical issues that affect us all… and therein hangs a tale… a very good tale.

Judith is available in person or on Skype to speak to your book group or at your library. As a minister and teacher, she is available to lead workshops and retreats on fiction, memoir, and spiritual biography. Please contact her and get on her mailing list through her website, www. judithcampbell-holymysteries.com, or through her two Facebook pages: Judith Campbell, and Judith Campbell Author. She loves to hear from her readers.